Behind bars . . . and innocent!

"Who's making all that noise?"

"It's the new girl. She's the troublemaker."

Jessica stopped and squinted into the darkened hallway outside her cell. "I'm not a troublemaker. I can't sleep."

"Guilty conscience." One of the voices snickered.

Jessica tossed back her blond hair, her eyes blazing. "I'm not guilty of anything," she proclaimed. "I shouldn't even be in here!"

"Oh, sure." Another woman laughed cruelly. "Then why did you break down crying in the cafeteria? Guilty, I say."

Jessica felt her face heating up. "That wasn't guilt," she shouted. "That was—I just felt so bad."

Two more voices erupted in laughter.

"Oh, poor baby," the same cruel voice sneered. "Feeling sorry for herself. Too weak and *guilty* to do anything but cry. Would rather give up than fight."

Jessica's mouth dropped open. *How dare they talk to me like that!* she fumed. She felt anger surging through her, wiping away any feelings of self-pity. She shot over to the bars of her cell. She'd show them. Jessica Wakefield had never given up on herself in her life. She was a strong person. She believed in herself.

She gripped the bars of her cell. "I am not weak!" she shouted. "I am n~~ot guilty!~~" ~~She clenched her~~ making them rattle. ~~"Jessica~~ Wakefield is innocent!~~"~~

D1380177

SWEET VALLEY UNIVERSITY®

The Trial of Jessica Wakefield

Written by
Laurie John

Created by
FRANCINE PASCAL

BANTAM BOOKS
NEW YORK · TORONTO · LONDON · SYDNEY · AUCKLAND

SWEET VALLEY UNIVERSITY:
THE TRIAL OF JESSICA WAKEFIELD
A BANTAM BOOK : 0 553 50514 9

Originally published in USA by Bantam Books

First publication in Great Britain

PRINTING HISTORY
Bantam edition published 1997

The trademarks "Sweet Valley" and "Sweet Valley University"
are owned by Francine Pascal and are used under license by
Bantam Books and Transworld Publishers Ltd.

Conceived by Francine Pascal

Produced by Daniel Weiss Associates, Inc,
33 West 17th Street, New York, NY 10011

Bantam Books are published by Transworld Publishers Ltd,
61–63 Uxbridge Road, London W5 5SA,
in Australia by Transworld Publishers (Australia) Pty Ltd,
15–25 Helles Avenue, Moorebank, NSW 2170,
and in New Zealand by Transworld Publishers (NZ) Ltd,
3 William Pickering Drive, Albany, Auckland.

Printed and bound in Great Britain by
Cox & Wyman Ltd, Reading, Berkshire.

To Justin Du Van

Chapter One

"Move one muscle and I'll handcuff you to that bench, blondie!" the beefy police matron barked as she shoved Jessica Wakefield.

Jessica cried out as she fell onto the rock-hard bench outside the interrogation room at the Sweet Valley Police Station. "I didn't do anything wrong!" she wailed. "Why are you treating me like this?"

The police matron cackled. "You'd better get used to it, sweetheart. This is how we treat drug dealers."

"But I'm not a drug dealer," Jessica protested, her voice cracking.

The matron sneered, crossing her large arms firmly in front of her chest. "From what I hear, you were about to sell a hundred grams of cocaine when you were busted last night."

"It was a mistake," Jessica sobbed, feeling what little control she had slipping away. "I didn't know—"

The matron cut her off with a growl. "Save it for the judge, blondie. Your sniveling excuses aren't going to get you anywhere here. Or in jail, which is where you're heading."

Jail! Jessica felt the blood drain from her face. This was a nightmare! There'd been a terrible mistake. Why wouldn't anyone believe her? Her heart began crashing against her chest, her breath coming in anxious gasps. In a minute she was going to faint. Jessica bent her head between the knees of her black leggings, her long blond hair swinging into her lap, and tried to steady herself. *Calm down, Jess,* a little voice inside her soothed. *Nick will believe you.*

"Nick," Jessica whispered, struggling to keep her fear from taking control. "Nick will straighten this out." *Or would he?* she wondered, a new surge of panic rising in her chest. It was Nick who'd slapped the cuffs on her wrists and pushed her into the police car last night. "Oh, Nick," she sobbed to herself, "why didn't you tell me the truth about who you really are?"

She shook her head as the shock of last night's discovery again ran through her mind. Nick wasn't a student and he wasn't a mysterious spy like in the fantasies she'd been having about him. He was an undercover police officer, working at SVU!

If only she'd known the truth, she never would have gone to the science building. And she wouldn't be in this mess. *Why didn't you tell me, Nick?* she thought desperately. *Why didn't you trust me?*

Loud footsteps and a familiar voice cut through her thoughts. Jessica snapped up her head to see Nick Fox in his battered motorcycle jacket and torn blue jeans striding down the hall toward her.

"Nick," Jessica cried, starting to her feet. "Thank goodness you're here! You've got to tell them. This is all a mistake—"

The matron clamped a heavy hand on her slender shoulder and roughly pushed her back down.

"It's OK, Marty," Nick said. "I'll take it from here."

Jessica felt the matron's tight grip relax through the thin cotton of her black turtleneck. "All right, Detective, but watch this one. She's been babbling all night. Don't turn your back on her. I think she might be a psycho."

Jessica glared at the beady-eyed matron indignantly. How dare she! If she'd been babbling, it was because the police officers had kept her up all night after the arrest—fingerprinting her, taking that horrible mug shot, and treating her like she was a piece of dirt.

But before she could respond, Nick grabbed her arm and roughly pulled her up. "Let's go, Jessica," he said in a wooden voice.

"Where, Nick?" Jessica cried. "Home?"

His bright, forest green eyes looked at her with cold contempt. "Only a judge can let you go home now. I'm taking you to a holding cell, where you'll wait until your bail hearing in the morning."

"But it is the morning," Jessica exclaimed, frantically searching the dreary gray walls for a clue to the time. She knew the police had kept her up all night. Her aquamarine eyes locked on the clock through the door of the interrogation room. "It's almost eight A.M.!"

"*Tomorrow* morning," Nick snapped back.

Jessica's mouth dropped open. "I can't spend another night here, Nick. You've got to help me. Can't you get me out of here?" She felt hot tears rushing to her eyes.

"Sorry, Jessica," Nick said tersely. "Unlike you, I don't make deals with druggies."

Jessica gasped, staring at him in horror. "Nick, what are you saying? I never made any drug deal." She couldn't believe her ears. Nick was the guy she loved. The guy she wanted to grow old with. "Why don't you believe me?"

"Believing in you was the biggest mistake I ever made, Jessica," Nick sneered, shaking his head. "I went to make a drug buy last night. To bust the person who's been pushing poison at SVU. The last person I expected to find waiting to make the sale was the woman I *thought* I loved. But that's over now. You won't fool me again."

Jessica felt as if a knife had been plunged into her heart. "Nick," she whimpered. "How can you say that?"

"Easy, druggie. Now get moving."

Jessica stumbled in a veil of tears as Nick led her through a maze of fluorescently lit hallways and then down a dingy flight of stairs to the basement level of the police station. Her ears were ringing from his brutal words and her heart was frozen in shock. This couldn't be the guy she loved. In a minute he'd change back into the Nick she'd known yesterday. He'd take her in his strong arms and tell her all of this was a bad dream.

"Lottie," Nick called, banging on a thick glass door covered with wire mesh. "I've got a prisoner."

The door buzzed open and Nick pushed her through. The woman named Lottie handed him a ring of keys. "Cell three is empty," she growled.

Nick pulled Jessica down the dark, musty hall toward the cell.

"Nick, please," Jessica wept, digging in the heels of her cowboy boots. "I'm scared."

"Keep it down," a harsh voice called from inside a darkened cell. "People are trying to sleep here."

Nick tugged at her arm. "You asked for this, Jessica, when you broke the law." He slid open the cell door.

"But I didn't mean to," Jessica sobbed, clinging to Nick's leather coat. "Why won't you believe me, Nick? Look at me . . . please. Can't you see it in my eyes? I love you and I'm telling you the truth."

He glared at her. "All I know is you were caught red-handed with enough cocaine to destroy a lot of lives."

"Let me explain," she pleaded. "I didn't know what was in that package. I thought—" Her words froze as Nick's icy green eyes bored into her.

"Save it for the judge."

Jessica felt the air go out of her lungs as if he'd punched her. *He's lost all respect for me*, she thought miserably. *He's not going to listen to what I have to say.*

"You're not the person I thought you were," Nick said, his voice sounding cold and harsh.

He gave her a soft push, propelling her into the tiny cell, where she sprawled across the single cot.

"No, Nick!" Jessica screamed, scrambling to her feet in one last attempt to get through to him. "Don't leave me! You've got to listen to me."

The face staring back at her was that of a stranger, his look as hard and unmoved as stone. Nick slid the cell door into place with a *clang*.

Jessica grabbed onto the cold steel bars as scalding tears streamed down her face. "Nick!" she screamed, her voice trailing away into anguished sobs as he disappeared down the darkened hallway. Jessica clung to the bars, her heart breaking as a wave of hopelessness overcame her. It was no good. Nick no longer loved her. She was completely alone.

Elizabeth Wakefield's slender hand shook as she punched out the familiar digits of Tom Watts's number on the telephone in her dorm room. A number she'd dialed a thousand times before over the past months, but never with such apprehension and anxiety.

"Please be there, Tom," she whispered as the phone began to ring. She had called him close to ten times that morning, leaving messages that had gone from sensible to near panic. *It's as if he's disappeared into thin air,* she thought. "Or more likely he's doing a great job of avoiding you, Liz," she told herself.

Elizabeth cringed. She and Tom had gone through rough patches before, but nothing as bad as last night. She closed her sea-green eyes tightly, the image of her hand slapping Tom's face playing over and over again in her mind's eye. The memory made her stomach twist and her face turn beet red with shame.

Elizabeth squeezed the phone. Everything had gone so terribly wrong since Mr. Conroy, Tom's newfound biological father, had arrived at SVU. First Mr. Conroy had made unwanted advances toward her. Then when she'd finally found the courage to tell Tom, the inconceivable had happened. Tom—the sensitive, loving guy she thought she could tell anything to— had refused to believe her. Instead he'd accused her of wanting to ruin his happiness, of being selfish and jealous of the time he spent with his new dad.

Elizabeth buried her face in her pillow, letting the receiver slip down beside her. "Tom didn't mean those things," she tried to assure herself, swallowing the hard lump in her throat. "He was just upset."

Tom always blamed himself for his family's tragic death while they were traveling to see him play in a football game. *Of course Tom doesn't want to believe that Mr. Conroy is less than perfect,* she thought, sitting up and twisting the hem of the white sailor top she wore over her slim black trousers. *Having found his biological father is like having a second chance at a family.*

"Hello—"

"Tom!" Elizabeth cried, diving for the phone and clutching it to her ear.

"This is Tom. Sorry I'm not home right now"—Tom's answering machine droned—"if you'd like to leave a message—"

Elizabeth grimaced at the sound of the tape as she pulled at a loose strand of long blond hair that had escaped from her ponytail. Now what? *I know you're there,* she thought. If he wouldn't answer, how could she ever get through to him?

The machine beeped. "Tom, please pick up. We have to talk," Elizabeth pleaded.

"Hello?" Tom's actual voice sounded sullen as it cut in on the answering machine.

"Tom," Elizabeth gushed, relief flooding her voice. "Is it really you? I've been calling all morning."

"What is it, Elizabeth?" His usually sexy voice came back sounding cold and distant.

Elizabeth took a deep breath and then plunged in. "I'm sorry, Tom, about everything that happened last night. I didn't mean to hurt you. I'd never want to do that. You've got to believe me."

"Right," Tom said sarcastically. "Slapping my face and telling me my father came on to you was supposed to make me feel like a million bucks. Is that it, Liz?"

Elizabeth hesitated. She had to tread carefully. Tom sounded even more upset now than he had last night. She'd never heard such antagonism in his voice before. If she wasn't careful, she might lose him altogether. "It was, um . . . my mistake," she stammered. "I didn't know what to do. I handled it all wrong."

Tom snorted. "That's the understatement of the year. I can't believe you're so threatened by my happiness that you'd make up lies about my father. I finally have a family, my *own* family, and you can't deal with it. Why is that, Liz? Afraid you'll be replaced? That I won't be so dependent on you anymore? Or maybe you just can't stand to share me with anyone, even my own father."

Elizabeth felt her head spinning. Where was Tom getting these ideas? She gritted her teeth and plowed on. "That's not fair. I didn't want to hurt you. Can't you understand that?"

"I understand everything, Liz. You're not the person I thought you were." Tom's icy tone had given way to something stronger. Elizabeth could almost see his handsome face twisted in anger.

"That's not true. I had something important to tell you and I handled it badly. I didn't know what else to do." Elizabeth knew she was walking through a minefield now. One false step and *boom!* "When I talked it over with Nina—"

"What?" Tom cut her off with an angry splutter. "You've been spreading that garbage around campus? How dare you? You've betrayed me in the worst possible way!"

Oh no. How could she have been so stupid? She knew she'd done the right thing in confiding to her closest friend about Mr. Conroy's behavior. *A victim of sexual harassment should never feel she has to keep quiet,* Elizabeth reminded herself. But she should have realized Tom was too irrational right now to acknowledge that.

"Tom, I'm sorry. But put yourself in my place—" she started.

"No, Liz!" His voice cut her off frigidly. "You put yourself in my place. Then you'll see why I can't ever forgive you or trust you again."

"Don't say that," Elizabeth cried. "This has gotten all messed up. You have to believe me. I would never do anything to hurt you."

"You couldn't have hurt me more if you'd shot a bullet through my heart," he spat.

Elizabeth gasped, instinctively clutching her

11

pillow to her stomach. "Tom, please, don't do this to us."

"Us?" Tom said flatly. "There's no 'us' anymore. You destroyed that last night."

Elizabeth tightened her grip on the phone, the color draining from her face. She was having trouble catching her breath. *How can this be happening?* she thought as panic began to rip through her body. *No matter what I say, he's moving further away.* "Please, Tom," she croaked. "Let me explain."

"I don't need to hear any more," he coldly interrupted. "I don't know if I can see you for a while."

"Tom," Elizabeth sobbed. "Don't do this. I've got to see you."

"No, Liz," he flatly refused. "I've made up my mind."

Elizabeth felt her slender body begin to shake as Tom's words sank in. *He's breaking up with me,* she thought. She couldn't let that happen. She had to see him and make him understand. She couldn't lose him. Her heart was pounding so hard, she could barely hear her words.

"You've got to see me," she pleaded. "You've got to. I'll go anywhere you want." The desperation was thick in her voice, but she didn't care. If he'd meet her, she knew she could make him understand.

12

There was a long silence and then his voice broke in, cold and distant. "I'll be outside the TV station in fifteen minutes. If you're there, I'll see you."

Elizabeth hung up the phone and curled up on the bed, her knees drawn up to her chest. "I'll be there," she whispered. "I'll do anything to keep us together."

"It's about time, Jordan," Celine Boudreaux snapped. She flung open the front door of her apartment to a pale, skinny guy with a face full of freckles and short white blond hair. "Where have you been all night?" *He'd better have a good excuse,* she thought, inhaling deeply from her cigarette. She'd been half out of her mind, worrying that the drug deal she'd so carefully orchestrated had gone sour. She let the smoke curl out of her mouth.

"Me?" Jordan Wilson countered, dropping a large pink-flowered hatbox on the floor. "You were supposed to meet me at the Java Joint after I made your secret document exchange or what-ever that was. I waited for you for over two hours."

Celine gave a dismissive shrug. "I got held up," she lied quickly. The truth was that she'd avoided the Java Joint in case Jordan was fol-lowed from the science building, where he was making the cocaine delivery. But she didn't think it would take until this morning to catch up to him.

"Forget that," Celine spat. She didn't have time to dither with Jordan. He had her money and she wanted it—now. She tugged at the hem of her short red negligee anxiously. "You did give my friend Nick the package full of papers, didn't you?"

"I gave someone something, all right, Celine," Jordan told her testily. "But it wasn't Nick. It was a girl and five minutes later she was surrounded by cops and arrested."

"What!" Celine gasped, pulling him into her tiny bedroom. The one room in that awful boardinghouse where her nosy neighbors couldn't eavesdrop. "Did you get my package?"

Jordan narrowed his sky blue eyes. "Is that all you care about? What about the fact that I could have been arrested?"

Celine gritted her teeth, angrily stabbing out her cigarette in the cut-glass ashtray on her bed. "Obviously you weren't arrested or you wouldn't be here, unless—" Celine's mind raced frantically. *Unless the police let him go so they could tail him!* Were they waiting outside right now?

She grabbed Jordan by the arms, shaking him. "How did you get away? Did anyone follow you?" she screeched.

Jordan yelped and jumped back from her. "Of course not," he cried. "I got away before anyone saw me. I hid and then I ran through the woods. But what's this all about? What was in those documents?"

"Never mind those," Celine snipped, tossing back her honey blond curls. "Did you get my package?" Everything was riding on that. If Jordan hadn't got the money from the drug deal, she was sunk.

"Yes," Jordan said indignantly. He retrieved the hatbox from the hallway and threw it on the bed.

Celine dove for it, yanking off the top and ripping the carefully folded tissue paper apart. She pulled out a large, floppy white hat, turned it inside and out, and tossed it to one side. Then she dug back into the box, rummaging through the tissue paper left on the bottom. "Where's the cash?" she hissed. She turned on Jordan, her porcelain cheeks molten with anger. "What did you do with my money?"

"What money?" Jordan asked.

"The drug money, you fool," Celine cried. "I gave you a hundred grams of cocaine and all you got was a stupid hat?"

"Drugs?" Jordan screamed, his eyes as wide as saucers. "I'm so stupid! I knew that story about illegal animal testing was a lie!"

"That's right, sweetheart," Celine barked. "Drugs. Now where's the money to pay for them?" She felt her stomach turning into butterflies. Some very scary people had given her that cocaine *on credit*. And not only that, she was counting on the money to pay for the redecoration of the parlor at Theta house, which she'd also paid for *on credit*. Those snooty girls hadn't made her a member just for her good looks; they were expecting a beautifully furnished room.

Jordan's chin began to quiver and his hands clenched into fists. "You used me!" he spluttered. "You made me a drug courier. I've got to go to the police!"

Celine leaped off her bed, not caring that she overturned an ashtray full of cigarette butts, and angrily seized Jordan by the shoulders. "You'll do no such thing!" she screeched, shaking him like a rag doll. Where did a nobody like Jordan get off talking to a Boudreaux like that?

"Wake up and smell the Chanel, Jordan. You're an accomplice now. You traded a hundred grams of cocaine for a floppy white hat. That makes you two things—an idiot and a criminal. Selling drugs, even for a hat, is an illegal transaction in this state. And if I go down, I'm taking you with me." She grabbed her red silk robe from the foot of her bed and wrapped it around herself.

"And the police are the least of your worries right now," she continued, her anger barely under control. "You were supposed to bring back cold, hard cash. There are some rather unpleasant men expecting that money. And in a couple of days they'll come looking for it. I'd hate to have to point them in your direction."

Jordan's face turned as white as a sheet. Even his freckles disappeared. "You wouldn't," he gasped.

Celine laughed and toyed with the tassel of her robe. "I certainly would, Jordie. But I'm sure we can come to some kind of understanding. You don't go to the police and I won't give your name to the mob. But you'd better figure out a way to come up with my money."

Jordan spluttered, struggling for words. "Me? Where am I going to get that kind of cash?"

Celine shrugged and smiled. "Rob a bank?"

Jordan's eyes nearly popped out of his head. "That's cr-crazy," he stammered. "This whole thing has nothing to do with me."

"Oh, I'm afraid you're wrong there." She fluttered her eyelashes and turned on her megawatt smile. "You're right in the middle of this little mud pie."

Jordan wrung his hands, choking back tears. "How could you do this to me? I . . . thought we had something special, Celine."

Celine's bottom lip curled in distaste as she

looked up at Jordan's hangdog face, his big, gullible eyes full of hurt. He seemed so upset, she actually felt a pang of emotion. *Guilt.* It had been a long time since she'd felt guilty about anything. And now she remembered—it was the emotion she hated most. *This won't do, Celine,* she thought. *You have your own skin to worry about.* Jordan had served his purpose. It was time for him to go.

"It was *special,* all right, Jordan," she crowed. "That's why I hope you come up with the money. But if not, I promise to wear my best little black dress to your funeral." She threw back her head, forcing herself to laugh. She kept laughing as his face crumpled into angry tears and he ran from the room.

Celine fell back on her bed with an exhausted groan. That was one problem out of the way. Now all she had to do was figure out how to come up with some cash. "It's not fair," she cried. "At this rate the credit card companies are going to repossess the furniture I ordered. I'll be kicked out of the Thetas before I even get to spend a night under their roof!" *Or worse,* she gloomily reminded herself. *If I don't get that cocaine money, I may end up lying at the bottom of the ocean in a pair of cement stilettos.*

Chapter Two

"Why are you doing this, Elizabeth?" Tom Watts muttered to himself as he stood on the grassy quad outside the WSVU campus TV station. "How could you betray me?" Beneath his blue polo shirt his powerful back muscles were aching with tension. He felt as if his whole world had been turned upside down. *I trusted you,* he thought. *How could I have been so wrong?* He reached out a hand to steady himself against the metal railing that ringed the building.

"He's been making passes at me, Tom." Elizabeth's words replayed in his mind, only now with a singsong hint of malice. "It started at the restaurant, when you were in the bathroom. . . ."

Tom closed his eyes. *She's blowing things out*

of proportion, he thought. His father liked her. Wasn't that what Tom had always told Elizabeth he wanted? To have a family that could love her as much as he did?

"He grabbed me and tried to kiss me." Elizabeth's words came back at him in a cruel taunt.

Tom shook his head. It couldn't be true. It couldn't!

"Your dad is a very sick man," she'd jeered.

"Lies," Tom screamed. "All lies." He grabbed his pounding head to keep it from splitting apart.

Two students who were strolling by looked over at him and then hurried on. He turned his back to them and caught a glimpse of his face in the reflection of the modern glass building. The dark eyes staring back at him were haunted, the mouth pinched with bitterness. *And why not?* he thought angrily. *The woman I love betrayed me.* First Elizabeth had helped his father find him. Now she was deliberately trying to tear them apart.

The last time he'd felt this mad was when he'd been told of his family's death. Then his anger had been directed at himself. Now, though, it was at someone who was trying to take his new family away from him. *I won't let you do it, Elizabeth,* he thought.

"Damn you, Liz!" he shouted out loud, pounding his fists against his sides. "You of all people. You were the one who brought me back from my despair over the death of my first family. How can you destroy this one?"

A flash of golden blond hair caught his eye. He turned, and Elizabeth came into view. Tom felt his stomach flip over, and he took a large gulp of air. A few days ago there hadn't been anybody but Elizabeth he'd wanted to see. Now the sight of her made his guts twist up so badly that he was afraid he might get sick. He turned his back to her, trying to push away the revulsion he felt. *You betrayed me, Liz,* he thought. *Why?*

Elizabeth could feel her hands shaking as she walked up the winding path to the entrance of WSVU. She'd never been this frightened in her life. Her and Tom's whole relationship depended on this meeting. She had to make Tom listen, get him to understand what had happened, or they were as good as broken up. She shoved her hands in the front pockets of her pants to keep them from fluttering. *Be brave, Liz,* she counseled herself. *It's Tom. You love each other.*

"There he is!" she whispered, spying Tom standing outside the station. Elizabeth nodded and smiled at him. But instead of acknowledging her, he turned his back and faced the building. Elizabeth felt her stomach sink, and her hands begin to shake even more. "It's OK," she told herself. *I'm going to stay calm and explain exactly what happened. Tom will see I'm telling the truth and everything will be fine.*

Tom spun around as she stepped up to him. His dark eyes were clouded, and his mouth was set in a grim line.

"Oh, Tom," she babbled, losing her composure at the sight of his pained face. "I'm sorry if I hurt you, but I didn't know what else to do. I had to say something. It was a horrible weight on me. I was afraid it would drive us apart. Please understand. I just knew I couldn't keep it from you."

Tom held up his hand for her to stop. "Just one question," he said through gritted teeth. "Do you really believe what you said about my father?"

Elizabeth hesitated, her mind racing frantically through her options. If she said no, then Tom would be hers again. She could almost feel his strong, warm arms around her body. Wasn't that worth almost any price? Even the dark shadow of Mr. Conroy? But if she were honest and said yes, maybe Tom *would* believe her. Then they could work out the problem together, the way they always had.

"Tom," she said softly. "Everything I told you is true."

Tom's lips seemed to tighten and shrink. He closed his eyes.

Elizabeth stared after him, terrified, her heart pounding in her ears. She held her breath, afraid that one wrong move, one wrong word would drive him away. She had never felt so isolated from him before.

It was ages before Tom opened his eyes. But when he did, his gaze was cold and lifeless. Elizabeth felt her hopes being crushed.

"Then I think this should be the last time we see each other," Tom said flatly.

Elizabeth felt as if she'd been punched. "You can't mean that," she insisted, her voice breaking. Memories of the good times and the love they'd shared flashed through her mind. Images of them laughing and falling into each other's arms stung her eyes. Her need for him to step forward and hold her was so strong, it was a physical ache. "You can't."

"Yes, I can," he replied, his face as hard as granite.

Elizabeth took a step toward him, knowing it was her last chance to break through. But Tom raised his hands and jumped back as if he were afraid.

Or repulsed, she thought, a sob escaping from her throat.

"We're not going to see each other anymore," Tom announced in his deadened voice. "It's over between us." He turned from her and walked slowly into the station.

Elizabeth felt a groan escape from her throat. A shuddering sob racked her body. "Tom!" she called after him. But he didn't turn around, and the TV station door closed behind him. "Tom!" she cried once more, barely able to see through the tears streaming down her face. "Don't do this," she moaned, her heart shattering like glass. Then she turned and ran blindly back toward her room.

Clang! Jessica jumped as the door of her cell slammed open and a tall, gaunt jailhouse matron stepped in. The matron bent toward her, and Jessica felt the woman's long, bony fingers wrap around her upper arm like claws.

"On your feet," the matron barked. A large nightstick hung from her thick black belt.

"What do you want with me?" Jessica gasped, recoiling from the woman's steely grip. "Am I going home now?"

The matron screwed her bony face up into a frightening half smile and laughed out loud. "Home? That's a good one. The only way you're

24

getting out of here is with a chisel and a hack-saw!"

Jessica choked back tears. She'd never felt so alone and forsaken in her life. "Is it Nick, then? Are you taking me to see him?" she asked, feeling a small glimmer of hope.

"Detective Fox?" the matron asked, wiping tears of laughter from her eyes. "Fat chance you'll ever see him again! I'm taking you to see your lawyer. Twenty minutes, then back in your cell."

"No," Jessica cried, no longer able to keep back her desperate tears. "That can't be true. Nick wouldn't abandon me like this. You've got to get him for me."

"Are *you* giving *me* an order?" the matron roared, grabbing Jessica roughly by the arm and yanking her to her feet.

Jessica cried out in terror. "No . . . I'm sorry . . . I—"

"Shut up!" the matron bellowed. "You're lucky I'm in a good mood today. But don't get out of line again or it's the hole for you. Where nobody can hear you scream!"

A few nasty cackles erupted from the cells around them.

All color drained from Jessica's face, and she began shaking uncontrollably.

"Now get moving." The matron dragged

Jessica up a flight of stairs to a long corridor. She opened one of the steel doors and pushed Jessica into a small, windowless room. Jessica nearly stumbled, catching herself on the back of a chair. She was face-to-face with a portly man in a rumpled gray suit and red bow tie. The man sat at a metal table, a battered briefcase and a yellow legal pad before him.

"Hello, Ms. Wakefield," he said, standing up and offering his pudgy hand over the table. "I'm Daniel Mills. I've been appointed by the court to represent you."

"You've got to get me out of here," Jessica whispered frantically as she clutched at his hand. "Please, I'm begging you." She jumped as the matron slammed the door shut behind her and slid home the bolt.

Mr. Mills nodded kindly, gently extracting his hand from her grip. "I'll do my best, Ms. Wakefield." He motioned to the chair across from him, waiting for Jessica before taking his own seat. "I know of your father," Mr. Mills told her. "He has a fine reputation in this town."

"My father?" Jessica cried. She didn't want her parents to know about the arrest. It would ruin their vacation. "Have you spoken to him already?"

Mr. Mills shook his head. "Not yet. As you

know, your parents are away in Australia, but I'll be trying to reach them as soon as we're done here."

"No!" Jessica said forcefully. As terrible as she felt, she'd only feel worse if they cut their trip short because of her. "I don't want my parents notified. They've been planning this vacation for months, and I don't want it spoiled over a mistake." Besides, by the time her parents got home, this would all be cleared up, right?

The lawyer nodded understandingly and made a note on his legal pad.

"But I would like you to call my brother, Steven, and my sister, Elizabeth," she added.

"Your brother and his girlfriend are already here. They're upstairs waiting to see you."

"Really?" Jessica said, brightening slightly. Since the arrest, she'd felt completely alone. Now she realized that her family and friends were probably doing everything they could to clear her name.

"Your brother's been upstairs all morning, trying to line up a bail bondsman," Mr. Mills informed her. "After your bail hearing tomorrow morning, we'll be in an excellent position to get you out of here."

Thank goodness. This whole experience was a nightmare. She didn't know who to be more afraid of, the matrons or the other prisoners.

The sooner she got out of here, the better.

"But how did Steven know I was in jail?" she asked. "I didn't think the call I made to him last night got through." She hoped her arrest wasn't on TV or the radio. *That would be too humiliating,* she thought. She slumped in the hard metal chair, wrapping her arms around her now filthy black turtleneck.

Mr. Mills nodded. "Apparently he heard enough on his answering machine to get him worried. Then he called the police in case you were in trouble."

Jessica closed her eyes. She could imagine the rest. "She's in trouble, all right." That mean desk sergeant had probably laughed. "That's why we've got her locked up!" Jessica shuddered and tried to put the image out of her mind.

"What about my sister, Elizabeth?" she asked hopefully. "Is she here too?"

Mr. Mills shook his head. "I don't believe so. Your brother mentioned that he hasn't been able to reach her."

"Liz," Jessica moaned, squeezing her eyes shut. Suddenly she had a feeling of what it would be like if she really had to go to jail—a heart-wrenching separation from her family and friends. But especially from her twin sister. It would be totally awful. She couldn't imagine life without Elizabeth.

Elizabeth had always been there for her, through thick and thin. Sure, they'd had their ups and downs, like all siblings. Even though they looked identical—with their slim, athletic bodies, long, golden blond hair and heart-shaped faces—their personalities were as different as night and day.

Jessica had always been the wilder of the two, more into adventure, good-looking guys, and fun. Elizabeth was the practical, serious one, more comfortable in stable, long-term relationships. But Elizabeth was the one who was invariably there to get Jessica out of a jam. And while Jessica hadn't always appreciated her sister's practical approach to life, especially when it threatened Jessica's good times, deep down she knew they shared a bond that could never be broken. If she had to live without Elizabeth, she didn't know if life would be worth living.

Mr. Mills cleared his throat, bringing Jessica back to the present and the dingy little room with its hard metal chairs. He pulled his legal pad toward him and uncapped his pen. "So tell me what happened."

Jessica recalled the blinding police spotlights and that chilling voice as it yelled, *"Freeze!"* Then she pictured Nick's scornful, disappointed face and couldn't go on. *Nick,* she thought, biting her lip. *I need you so badly. Why aren't you*

29

here with me? She dropped her head in her hands. "What's the use?" she said hopelessly. "No one's going to believe me. I'm going to spend the rest of my life in jail."

Elizabeth sniffed back a tear and reached out a shaky hand to unlock the door of her dorm room at Dickenson Hall.

At that moment she heard her phone ring, startling her and causing the key to fall from her hand.

"Oh no," she cried, dropping to her knees to retrieve it. "It might be Tom!" She grabbed the key and fumbled at the lock as the phone continued to ring. Finally the tumbler clicked, and she flung open the door. "Hello," she gasped.

"Liz." Her heart fell. It wasn't Tom at all. It was her brother, Steven. "I've got some bad news," he said, his voice sounding very subdued.

Elizabeth dropped down onto her bed, gripping the phone tightly. She was afraid a fresh batch of sobs might escape at any moment. *What now?* she thought. After her disastrous meeting with Tom, she doubted she could take much more. "What is it?" she whispered.

"I'm at the police station. Jess has been arrested." Steven moaned. "She's being held in the Sweet Valley jail."

Elizabeth leaped up. "Arrested!" Any thoughts of Tom immediately flew from her mind. Her twin sister was in trouble. "What happened?"

"She was busted in a police sting with over a hundred grams of cocaine."

Elizabeth's mouth dropped open. "Cocaine? That's impossible. Jessica would never have anything to do with drugs."

"I know," Steven agreed. "But the evidence is practically airtight."

"What do you mean?" Elizabeth asked. Everything was happening way too fast.

"The police think she's a drug dealer," Steven said incredulously. "They set up an undercover operation at SVU and she walked right into it. They caught her with the drugs in her hands."

Elizabeth shook her head, trying to clear her thoughts and make sense of what Steven was saying. There was no way Jessica would knowingly be involved with drugs. Jessica felt the same way about them that Elizabeth and Steven did. Drugs were poison. Elizabeth steadied herself on the side of her dresser. "Steven, we both know that's impossible. How did it happen?"

Steven sighed. "I don't know. I haven't been able to see her yet, and she's not cooperating with her public attorney. He told me she wouldn't answer his questions. Apparently she's convinced that she's going to be convicted no matter what she says."

"Poor Jessica." Elizabeth groaned. "She must be terrified." Elizabeth knew it took a lot to make her sister clam up. "When did this happen?"

"Last night," Steven replied.

Elizabeth gasped. "Last night?" That meant that while Elizabeth had been preoccupied with her relationship with Tom, Jessica had been locked up in a jail cell! And here Elizabeth had assumed Jessica was out dancing the night away or staying over with one of her sorority sisters at Theta house. "Oh, Steven, I've been such a terrible sister. I should have been with her last night."

"Don't worry about it," Steven assured her. "There's nothing you could have done. But I think you should get down here right away. Maybe you can talk some sense into her. She's got to start cooperating with her lawyer or she'll never get out of jail."

"I'll be right there," she promised.

Elizabeth hung up the phone and ran directly to her sister's closet. Knowing Jessica, she thought, after a night in a jail cell she'd be screaming for a fresh change of clothing. Elizabeth selected a pair of lace undies, sturdy blue jeans, and a thick, burgundy sweatshirt, which she shoved into her sister's carryall, along with some basic toiletries.

"Jessica might have to appear in court," Elizabeth reminded herself. She turned to her own closet and pulled out a sensible tan suit and a white, high-collared blouse. Clothes way too dull for Jessica under normal circumstances. "Sorry, Jess," she said, wincing as she imagined her sister's rolling eyes when she saw the suit. "But these are definitely *not* normal circumstances."

"What's going on?" Alexandra Rollins asked as she skipped up the stairs to the Theta house porch. There was a delivery van parked outside, and two burly-looking men were unloading a large blue couch.

Isabella Ricci was sitting on the porch swing, her beautiful face twisted in displeasure. "Celine's sorority dues," she snarled, her voice thick with sarcasm. "She's having the new furniture for the parlor delivered this morning."

Alex groaned and slumped down next to her. She'd forgotten all about Celine and her plans to redecorate the Theta parlor. "It's not fair," Alex complained, running a hand through her thick auburn hair. "Being a Theta used to mean something."

"Tell me about it," Isabella replied. "I'm just afraid Celine is going to do something outrageous and make us all look like fools."

Suddenly the sickly sweet smell of overripe flowers wafted onto the porch. "Did I hear someone mention little ol' me?" Celine asked, popping up from around the far side of the porch, a cloud of her trademark gardenia perfume thick around her.

Isabella rolled her clear gray eyes. "I've got to go," she sneered. "I think I smell a rat." She stalked off into the house.

Celine shrugged. "That girl should get her phobias under control."

Alex made a face and started to get up herself. Seeing Celine parading around Theta house was a definite downer. When Alex was asked to join the Thetas, it had been one of the most exciting things to happen to her since coming to SVU.

The idea that a catty, devious, vicious person like Celine could waltz into the sorority by pledging to refurbish a room was sickening. It cheapened the whole Theta experience and even made Alex want to reach for a drink, a definite no-no where she was concerned. Alcohol was something Alex struggled with, but luckily, since she'd volunteered at the SVU substance-abuse hot line, her craving had become a lot easier to deal with.

"Don't hurry off so fast," Celine purred, taking the seat Isabella had vacated.

Alex drew a deep breath and almost choked on the heavy perfume. "What do you want, Celine?" she asked coldly.

"Nothing special." Celine smiled, flashing her perfect white teeth. "I just thought that now that we're sisters, we should become friends too."

Fat chance, Alex thought, adjusting the strap on her bright yellow sundress. The only time Celine was friendly was when she wanted something.

Just then two additional movers stomped up the stairs toward the porch. *Or at least I think they're movers.* Alex frowned. They were as big and muscular as the other men. But these guys weren't wearing overalls. One had on a navy blue pea coat and a blue stocking cap covering his head and the other was wearing a sharp-looking suit. Alex shuddered as she noticed the ugly scar that ran down the better-dressed man's cheek.

Celine gave out a little yelp and pushed herself back into the swing. Alex turned to her and watched as the color drained from her face. "What is it, Celine?" she asked. "Who are those guys?"

Celine's bottom lip trembled as she tried to

smile. "Nobody important," she squeaked. "Please excuse me." She got up and walked woodenly toward the two men.

What's wrong with this picture? Alex thought. The men looked more like thugs to her than movers. "Maybe there's something wrong with the furniture," she murmured, feeling the morning begin to brighten again. With any luck the parlor redecoration would blow up in Celine's face and she'd be kicked out of the Thetas!

Oh no! Celine thought, her blood running cold at the sight of the two men coming toward her.

She recognized the man in the pea coat and stocking cap immediately as her drug connection from the dock. The other man with the scar, she couldn't be sure of. It had been dark on the boat the night she'd picked up the cocaine, and they'd kept a flashlight glaring in her eyes much of the time.

Celine glanced around quickly. She could run for the door to Theta house or jump over the railing of the porch to escape. But in her skintight miniskirt and six-inch heels, neither offered a very appealing option.

No choice, she thought. *I'll have to bluff them.* Celine forced her terrified legs to make the short journey across the porch to where the two men were now standing.

"Gentlemen," she cooed, desperately trying to keep her pounding heart from bursting through her chest. "I wasn't expecting to see you so soon."

"We hope this isn't an inconvenient time, Celine," the man with the scar said smoothly.

Celine grimaced inwardly. She recognized the cultivated voice from the boat. He was the boss. The one with the power to have her killed.

"Not—not at all," Celine stammered, trying to maintain some control. "But it's not the end of the week already, is it?" She forced out a brittle laugh.

The man with the scar smiled unpleasantly. "We heard some bad news this morning. A drug bust on campus. We were hoping it didn't have anything to do with you."

"Me?" Celine croaked, wrapping her arms around her thin top in an attempt to keep herself from shaking. "This is the first I've heard of it."

"That's good, Celine," Scarface said. "Because if it turned out you lost the merchandise in some careless way and couldn't pay us back—" He reached into the pocket of his gray suit and pulled out a pearl-handled object. With a flick of his finger a long, shiny blade leaped out. He held up the knife, the thin blade glinting as it caught the morning sunlight. "I'd hate to have to ruin that pretty face of yours."

Celine gasped and her hands flew up to her cheeks.

Scarface laughed, the cruel look in his eyes positively homicidal. "Don't worry, beautiful," he said with a sigh. "It only hurts for a minute. Believe me, I know." He leaned toward her, showing off the jagged scar that ran down his own face. "Then it will all be over." He drew his index finger across his throat.

Celine felt her knees buckle, and she grabbed the porch railing for support.

"See you in five days, beautiful." The man in the pea coat laughed. "We can't wait to see how everything turns out."

Nick gunned the engine of his vintage motorcycle, feeling the vibration of the bike through his large, strong hands. The big 1963 Triumph was his pride and joy, and it was good to be back on it. Now that they'd made an arrest at SVU, he didn't have to pretend to be a student anymore. He'd moved back into his own apartment and could drive his bike instead of the Camaro whenever he wanted.

But today he was going to forget all about work, all about SVU, and especially all about

Jessica, the woman who'd deceived him and turned him into a fool. He was going to leave the whole world behind and lose himself in the thrill of speed. *It's me and the road,* he thought furiously, *and that's all!*

Nick eyed the traffic light in anticipation, timing the change to green perfectly. He let up on the clutch and opened the throttle wide, leaving the cars waiting at the light far behind him.

He sped up the highway, deftly shifting gears as he headed into a sharp turn. The bike groaned beneath him as he hugged the road dangerously close. "I don't care!" he shouted over the roar of the motor.

He raced toward the mountains, weaving in and out of traffic, passing cars as if they were standing still. The wind whipped at his leather jacket and chafed at the slight stubble that covered his hard, chiseled features. He almost overshot the turnoff for Dead Man's Pass and had to stand on his brakes, kicking up gravel and spinning dangerously close to a wipeout. But still he pushed his luck. Throwing himself down low over the chrome insignia on the gas tank, he pushed the bike to the limit, reaching sixty, seventy, eighty miles per hour. Now he was flying over the narrow road, heading up into the hills that ran along the coast.

"Drive," he told himself. "Just go and keep

on going." Anything to keep his mind occupied. Anything to keep his mind off . . . Jessica. Unbeckoned, her face floated across his consciousness. He bit down hard on his lip. "How could I have been so blind?" he shouted into the wind. He'd fallen in love with a drug dealer.

He'd been working undercover for three years and had one of the best arrest records in the department. He'd even been commended by the chief for his shrewd sense of character. *But then along came a spider,* he thought bitterly, *who twisted my heart around her little finger.* No one had ever pulled the wool over his eyes the way Jessica Wakefield had.

"Jessica," he spat angrily. "How did you slip under my radar?" He pushed the motorcycle even harder. The frame was shaking now, the noise from the straining motor howling in his ears. He knew he was on the edge of losing control, but he didn't care. *Jessica, why did you do this to me?* his mind shouted.

Suddenly the road narrowed and a sharp curve appeared before him. To his right was a steep, granite wall and to his left a drop of over five hundred feet into the crashing surf of the Pacific Ocean. No choice now. *Gotta make that turn, Nick.* He pumped his brakes, fearful of a skid-out, and pulled back on the throttle as much as he dared. Still he was flying toward the turn way too fast.

He clung to the bike, practically wrapping his muscular limbs around it, and threw his body weight to the left side. Only by laying the bike as close to the ground as possible could he navigate the turn. He hunched over one more inch, his knee all but kissing the pavement as the road flew beneath him. *Hold it steady!* One false move and he and the bike were going for a long, serious dive.

"I'm going down!" he screamed. He felt his powerful hands begin to relax. He was blacking out. He knew the symptoms. His mind was trying to make it easy for his body to let go of the handlebars and accept the plunge. *I'm not going to make it,* he thought.

Suddenly Jessica's tear-stained face flashed across his consciousness. "Don't leave me!" she pleaded from her jail cell. At the last possible moment he gripped the handlebars. "I won't leave you, Jess," he cried, pulling up the bike and clearing the turn by a fraction of an inch.

Nick skidded to a stop at the edge of a scenic overlook to catch his breath. Below him the Pacific's mighty surf crashed noisily onto the rocky beach. He dismounted the bike, legs shaking, and pulled off his helmet. *That was close!*

He walked over to a picnic bench beside the low stone wall and collapsed on top of it. Thoughts of Jessica came flooding back to him.

Her sparkling blue-green eyes, her shining blond hair, the dimple in her left cheek when she looked up at him and smiled. He thought back to the utter lack of comprehension on Jessica's beautiful face when they'd arrested her last night. Could anyone be that good an actress?

Nick shook his head. "But face the facts," he whispered to himself. "You went to meet a dealer last night and found Jessica there with the drugs in her hand." Two and two still equaled four. *Maybe you can't live with the way she fooled you.*

He scuffed the sole of his boot on the seat of the picnic table. Something didn't feel right. Even though he was a trained professional, he'd had trouble staying in character around Jessica. If she was fooling him, then she must be the most cold-hearted manipulator in the world. *Admit it, Nick,* he thought, *you've fallen for Jessica like a ton of bricks.*

Nick exhaled harshly and walked back to his motorcycle. No more running away. He was heading back to Sweet Valley, nice and easy, to talk to Jessica and give her a chance to explain. He owed her that much. *You owe it to yourself too,* he thought. *Because right now Jessica has your heart in her hands and it's breaking in two. And it's going to keep on breaking until you know the truth.*

Chapter
Three

The barred door creaked open with a groan. Elizabeth hesitated before she stepped into the tiny cell where her sister was being held. Jessica threw herself into Elizabeth's arms.

"I—I didn't do it," Jessica stammered, her face soaked with tears. "I'm not a drug dealer. Please, someone's got to believe me."

Elizabeth felt a sharp lurch in her heart and bit down on her lip to keep from crying out. Seeing her sister's trembling body and pale, drawn face ripped her apart inside. But collapsing into tears wouldn't help either of them. "I know," she murmured gently, leading Jessica to the narrow cot. "I believe you."

"It was all a major misunderstanding," Jessica sobbed, clinging to Elizabeth as they collapsed onto the thin mattress. "I didn't know what was in the package."

Elizabeth stroked her sister's hair. "Tell me what happened."

"I overheard him—I took the package. I— I . . ." She gasped.

"Jessica," Elizabeth said sharply. She had to get her sister thinking rationally. "Slow down. Now start at the beginning."

Jessica nodded and took a deep breath. "I'll try." She wiped her face dry with her sleeve. "OK. Nick's always been mysterious. That's what attracted me. Well, it was one of the reasons." She gave a small smile.

Elizabeth nodded. She could imagine the rest. Over the past weeks Jessica had gone on and on about Nick and how exciting he was to be with. There was the story of Nick and the dangerous car chase. Nick subduing a robber at the movie theater. Nick and his mysterious connections. Elizabeth winced. *Maybe I should have paid more attention,* she thought. *I could have saved Jess this heartache.*

"But I was dying of curiosity," Jessica continued. "Why all the secrets? You know how I get."

Elizabeth took her sister's hand, groaning inwardly. "I know."

Jessica's bottom lip began to quiver, and she wiped a tear from the corner of her eye with a shaky finger. "I knew Nick had a secret meeting arranged. I showed up instead of him."

Elizabeth's eyes widened. "And—"

Jessica shook her head. "When I got there, a guy handed me a package. I thought it would hold the answers to all Nick's secrets . . . so I took it."

"Jessica," Elizabeth gasped. *Didn't she realize the danger?*

"I had to," Jessica cut in. "Nick wouldn't tell me anything about himself. I thought my going to his rendezvous and opening the package would make everything clear. I did it for love!" Fresh sobs escaped from her sister's throat.

Elizabeth gave a deep sigh and wrapped her arm around her sister. "Don't worry, Jess," she murmured. "We'll get you out of here. We're doing everything we can."

Jessica squeezed her tightly. "All I want is to come home," she whimpered. "But if I'm ever going to get out of here, I need you to talk to Nick, explain to him that I would never have anything to do with drugs. He's got to believe me. Without Nick on my side the evidence is airtight. He's the only person who can really help me."

Elizabeth nodded solemnly. "I'll tell him."

"Thanks." Jessica smiled faintly, a little color returning to her cheeks. "But Liz," she said, her sea green eyes suddenly worried. "Why arc your eyes so swollen? What's going on?"

Elizabeth grimaced and felt a surge of fresh tears threatening the edge of her eyelids. More than anything she wanted to throw herself into Jessica's arms and tell her all about Tom. Her twin sister was the one person who could ease her pain. She hesitated, her bottom lip trembling. It would be so easy to blurt everything out. *No, Liz,* she admonished herself, keeping her back straight and her eyes dry. *Jess has enough problems to worry about now.*

"I'm fine, Jess," Elizabeth said, forcing a smile. "I'm just upset about you being in this place."

"Oh, Liz," Jessica cried, throwing her arms around Elizabeth. "I really did get into a mess."

Elizabeth hugged her sister tightly. Suddenly a loud crack made them both jump. The matron had banged her club on the bars. "That's enough," she barked. "Visiting hour is over."

Both girls stood up.

"I almost forgot," Elizabeth told her, wiping a stray tear from her cheek. "I brought you some clothes and your shampoo and makeup. The guards have it." She made a face. "They're checking everything for weapons."

Jessica shook her head. "Figures. I might as well be Al Capone in here."

Elizabeth stepped forward, and she and Jessica wrapped their arms around each other once more.

"I said out! Now!" the matron screamed from behind them.

Still Elizabeth and Jessica clung to each other.

"Lottie, I have a situation here," the matron screeched.

Elizabeth heard the heavy footsteps of two additional matrons running toward them. Then strong fingers bit into her flesh as the jailers pried her and Jessica from each other's arms.

"Hey, kid." A gruff voice cut through Jessica's despair. "Crying isn't going to get you anywhere."

Jessica squinted through her swollen eyes. But all she saw was her lonely, empty cell. "Who's there?" she whispered.

"Your neighbor," the voice told her. "You've been crying for hours. I didn't think there were that many tears in the world."

Jessica sat up on her bunk. The voice was harsh, but the tone was kind. "I can't help it," Jessica whimpered, her bottom lip trembling as fresh tears threatened to start up. "I'm so alone. The guy I love has totally turned his back on me. I've never been so miserable in my life."

"Hey, you don't have to tell me," her neighbor

said. "I'm right next door. I've heard everything you've said since they brought you in. Tough break having your boyfriend slap the cuffs on you. I wouldn't waste a teardrop on him."

"But I love him," Jessica wailed. "I love him so much. Why won't he help me?"

"I can't say, kid. But you'd be better off getting some sleep than lying there crying over him."

Jessica shook her head. "I'm too scared to sleep," she moaned. "I'm so tired. But every time I close my eyes, I think I hear something." She shuddered and wrapped her arms across her chest. "I'm afraid to fall asleep. I'm afraid—"

"It's OK, kid." Suddenly a hand appeared in front of Jessica's cell door. "Marian Banks," the voice attached to the hand said.

Jessica leaned forward and shook the hand. "Jessica Wakefield." The woman wore a beautiful ring with a red garnet in its center.

"What are you in for, Wakefield?"

"Cocaine possession," Jessica said glumly, leaning her head against the bars of her cell.

"That's a tough one. Never was into drugs myself," Marian told her.

Jessica heard the creaking of Marian's cot as she sat down.

"I'm not either. It's all a big mistake."

Marian laughed. "That's what they all say."

"I'm serious," Jessica exploded, clinging to the bars. "I think drugs are totally horrible. I would never have anything to do with them."

"OK, OK!" Marian exclaimed. "But calm down. You'll get the matron in here if you keep that up."

Jessica hung her head and sat down on her cot. "I'm sorry. I feel so helpless. I really had nothing to do with it, but no one believes me."

"I know what you mean," Marian agreed. "I'm in the same boat. My old man used to use me as his punching bag when he got drunk. Night before last I'd finally had enough of it and punched back. Now he's in the hospital and I'm in jail for attempted murder."

Jessica's mouth dropped open. "But it was self-defense!"

"Try telling that to Judge Dodd. If he had it his way, he'd bring back spitting as a capital offense!"

Jessica gasped. She hoped she wouldn't be brought before Judge Dodd, whoever he was.

"Anyway, kid, don't worry about falling asleep tonight." Marian yawned. "Nothing bad is going down. And it helps the time pass."

Jessica sighed and stretched out on her lumpy mattress, closing her exhausted eyes. *Maybe Marian's right,* she thought. If she slept long enough, maybe this would just go away.

*   *   *

Tom threw himself down on the single bed in his dorm room. He was sick and tired of pacing but too wound up to sleep. He punched his pillow to fluff it up and shoved it under his head, his eyes locked on the blank white ceiling. But there was nothing there to keep his attention. And without something to focus his mind on, his thoughts kept wandering back to Elizabeth. He yanked his eyes away and stared over at the blank screen of his computer.

"That history paper's due tomorrow, Watts," he reminded himself. "You could write that to kill some time." But it was no good; his motivation was sapped. He didn't feel like doing any work. In fact, he didn't feel like doing anything at all. He glanced at the clock. It was after ten P.M. Maybe he *should* just go to sleep.

He kicked at the stack of library books piled on the corner of his bed and watched as they tumbled over, fanning out across his dorm-room floor.

"Good one, Tom," he scolded himself. "What are you going to do for an encore, rip out their pages?"

Suddenly the door flew open and Danny Wyatt, Tom's roommate, burst in. "Tom, I just heard about you and Liz. Is it true?"

Tom jumped to his feet. *Has she spread it*

around campus already? he thought angrily. "It's true," he growled, leaning against his desk and crossing his arms.

"I can't believe it," Danny stated, his handsome African American features clouded with concern. He dumped his knapsack on his bed. "I always thought you and Liz were the perfect couple."

Tom scowled. "We all make mistakes."

"I know," Danny continued, his brows knit in confusion. "But you and Liz were practically an SVU institution."

Tom narrowed his eyes. *Why doesn't Danny drop it?* he thought. *Can't he see I don't want to talk about this?*

Danny tossed his jacket on his desk chair. "I mean . . . Liz is great. It's just a squabble, right? I bet you two will be back together by the end of the week."

Tom felt a throbbing start up at the base of his skull. "No chance," he said between gritted teeth. "She's not who I thought she was. She's a selfish, jealous liar."

Danny frowned and pulled off his striped polo shirt to get ready for bed. "That doesn't sound like Liz. Are you sure there wasn't some sort of misunderstanding?"

Tom could feel his anger bubbling up inside him. "Misunderstanding?" he hissed. "I'll say.

51

She accused my father of coming on to her."

Danny took a step back in the cluttered dorm room as if Tom had pushed him. "What?" he said, sounding shocked. "That's unbelievable. Have you talked to your father? I mean, maybe there was some misinterpretation of actions."

Tom clenched his hands into fists and glared at Danny. "My father would never come on to Elizabeth," he snapped. "Ever."

Danny made a face and took another step back. "I'm not making any judgments. You know him better than I do. I just wondered if you've talked to him. Maybe he has a sense of why Liz made the accusations."

Tom could feel hot blood flushing his cheeks. "My father—" he started, trying desperately to control the anger he felt roaring to the surface. But it was no good. He turned his face away in fury, his fists shaking. "Is the whole world conspiring to take my family away?" he shouted. "Or is it only the people closest to me?"

Danny's mouth dropped open. "Tom, I didn't mean—"

"Forget it," Tom cut him off, pushing past Danny toward the door. "Forget this whole conversation." He stalked out into the night before Danny had a chance to utter another damning word.

*   *   *

Nick checked his gun with the front-desk sergeant and then proceeded down the stairs to the women's section of the jail.

"Yo, Detective, how's tricks?" joked Marty, the night matron, fixing her beady brown eyes on him. "Here to see blondie? I'll be glad to give you a hand if you want to beat a confession out of her."

Nick laughed and handed her his leather jacket. Marty talked tough to keep her prisoners in line, but inside she was a big softie. Not like some of the other matrons who worked down there. "No," Nick scoffed. "But thanks for the offer."

Marty grinned her lopsided smile, her tiny eyes disappearing behind plump cheeks, and tossed him the keys to Jessica's cell door.

Nick walked silently down the dark, musty corridor on the rubber soles of his sneakers. It was after eleven P.M.; visiting hours were long over and most of the prisoners were sleeping. Nick stopped in front of Jessica's barred door and looked in. She was lying on the tiny cot, her long blond hair fanned about her head. A slim arm, clothed in a burgundy sweatshirt, lay across her face, covering her eyes. His heart did a flip-flop at her vulnerable appearance, and a soft smile curled on his lips. She shifted on the bed,

53

and he quickly rearranged his features into a steely mask.

"Jessica," he said harshly.

She scooted to a sitting position and sat huddled against the wall, her aquamarine eyes flashing in fright. When she saw it was him, though, relief flooded her features. "Nick," she cried. "You came!"

He unlocked the door and stepped into the cell.

Jessica began to stand, reaching for him. "I knew you wouldn't leave me."

"Stay where you are," he commanded. He leaned against the opposite wall and crossed his arms.

"Nick," Jessica moaned, sinking back onto the cot. "Why are you here, then?" She gazed up at him, her eyes wide.

He felt his throat catch and quickly cleared it. "I want you to tell me what happened."

"Why?" Jessica asked, tears building in her eyes. "You didn't want to hear it yesterday."

Nick shrugged, playing it cool. "You're right. I'm probably wasting my time." He made a move toward the door.

"No, Nick, wait," Jessica cried, jumping toward him and grabbing the sleeve of his flannel shirt.

Nick closed his eyes for a second. The feel of

her touch was like a high-powered electric current snaking through his body. He steeled himself against the powerful emotions he felt surging through his chest. Brutally he pulled away from her, desperately trying to disguise his feelings. "Are you ready to talk?"

Jessica jumped back as if she'd been stung and nodded.

"Then sit down."

Jessica slid down onto the cot, wrapping her arms around herself. Her eyes brimmed with tears.

He forced himself to look away. "Why were you at the science building parking lot?" he asked between gritted teeth.

Jessica gulped. "I knew that's where you were supposed to be."

Nick raised an eyebrow. "Because you were my connection? You knew I'd be at the science building because your middleman set it up that way?"

"No, Nick," Jessica stated, shaking her head. "I overheard your conversation on the phone when you were sunning yourself on the quad."

Nick thought back to that day. He'd been catching some rays on the grass outside the library. But Jessica had come up to him after he'd finished his call, not before. "How?" he asked.

She blushed a deep crimson. "I was hiding behind a tree."

"What?" Nick erupted.

"I was trying to find out what you were all about."

Nick made a face. Knowing how inquisitive Jessica was, she might be telling the truth. But he'd wait till he heard the rest of the story before making up his mind. "Then what?"

Jessica cringed. "I pulled the spark plug out of your car."

Nick shook his head. "That I don't believe."

"I was married to a mechanic," she said in a small voice. "I used the socket wrench from your tool kit."

He rolled his eyes. "Go on."

Jessica pulled up a corner of the thin blanket covering her cot and started twisting it between her hands. "I went to your meeting and a guy was there. He gave me a package and I gave him my friend Lila Fowler's hatbox. Then I walked into the parking lot and, well . . . you know what happened next."

Nick stared down at her. "Why? Why would you take a package meant for me?"

Jessica sighed. "I thought that whatever was in the package would tell me all about you. Don't you see, Nick? You've been so secretive."

Nick shook off her explanation. "Nobody

saw another guy, Jessica. Nobody saw anyone but you walking out of the shadows with a hundred grams of cocaine in your possession."

"But it wasn't mine, Nick!" Jessica cried. "You've got to believe me. I got it from some guy."

Nick narrowed his eyes. "And what did this guy look like?"

Jessica shook her head. "I don't know. It was dark. I can't remember. Why don't you believe me?"

Nick snorted. "A mystery man is very convenient, Jessica."

She clutched the blanket to her chest, her eyes wide and begging. "I'm not making it up. I swear it's the truth. He was there."

Nick looked away. He wanted nothing more than to believe her. But until he had some concrete proof, her story wasn't going to help either of them. And to find that proof, he'd have to remain a professional.

"Well, Jessica," he said cautiously, "that's an interesting story. But I don't know if I should believe it. That's going to be hard to decide." He didn't dare tell Jessica he planned to investigate her story. If she was telling the truth, he didn't want to raise false hopes that he could get her off. And if she was lying, he wasn't going to give her the satisfaction of having fooled him twice.

"You must believe it," Jessica pleaded, her voice breaking. "It's the truth. Please, Nick, look at me. Can't you see I'm telling you the truth?"

Nick allowed himself one glance at her tear-stained face before turning away, pulling Jessica's cell door closed behind him. He couldn't bear to stand there witnessing her pain, not with his own heart breaking.

He walked slowly down the corridor of cells toward the exit, the sound of Jessica's quiet crying echoing behind him. *I'm a detective,* he thought, roughly brushing away his own bitter tears. *I'll find out the truth, somehow.*

Chapter Four

"Move it," a large policewoman ordered, shoving Jessica roughly into the Sweet Valley courtroom. "Your lawyer should be here shortly."

Jessica stumbled to her seat, exhausted from her poor night's sleep in the jail and her daybreak wake-up call to make this early morning court appearance. Not only was she terrified, but her cheeks were burning from the humiliation. Anyone who'd seen her being escorted into the Sweet Valley courtroom by the two armed policewomen would think she was some kind of criminal. "But that's exactly what they think you are," she whispered to herself, tears threatening to spill from her eyes. *A cocaine criminal!*

She looked up to see Mr. Mills threading his way toward her through the cramped benches.

"Ms. Wakefield," he said, taking her hand. "How are you holding up this morning?" He was slightly out of breath and looked like he was wearing the same gray suit he'd had on the day before. Only now the suit looked even more rumpled and his red bow tie was slightly askew.

"Not very well," Jessica said, her voice frail and shaky. "I really want to go home." Her bottom lip trembled and a few tears began to fall. "I'm scared."

Mr. Mills patted the sleeve of the tan linen suit Elizabeth had lent her for her court appearance and sat down next to her. "Don't give up hope. With any luck you should be out on bail by this afternoon."

Jessica sighed deeply, feeling a tiny bit better, and took a nervous peek around the boisterous courtroom. She'd expected the court to be somber, but the room was noisy and crowded. The long dark benches were packed with defendants, lawyers, and dozens of spectators. She turned and spied Elizabeth, Steven, and Billie a few rows behind her. All three of them waved and gave her a thumbs-up sign. Farther back she could see her best friend, Lila Fowler, who gave her an encouraging smile. Next to Lila sat her Theta sisters Alex and Isabella. Jessica felt a warm glow in her chest. It felt good to have people who cared about her.

She began to scan the other side of the courtroom and almost immediately her eyes locked with Nick's. Jessica sucked in her breath as his cold green eyes held hers, staring intently at her for a moment before breaking away. What was he thinking?

"Please, Nick," she whispered desperately. "If you really love me, do something. Get me out of this mess."

"That's the judge." Mr. Mills broke into her thoughts, pointing to the massive mahogany bench at the front of the room. Jessica tore her eyes away from Nick's impassive face. The judge wore black robes offset by a shock of white hair perched atop his head. He peered down at the courtroom from behind half-rimmed glasses like a tiny bird. *He looks like someone's grandfather,* Jessica thought with relief. *This won't be so bad.*

"I've spoken with your sister, Elizabeth," Mr. Mills added, extracting a pad from his briefcase and consulting his notes. "I wish you'd told me earlier that a man gave you that package." He gave her an encouraging smile. "If you didn't know the contents, it puts an entirely new light on your case."

Jessica sat up. "It does?" she asked, feeling a sense of hope rise inside her. "Even though I was arrested with the cocaine?" The evidence seemed airtight to her.

"Absolutely," Mr. Mills replied, straightening his bow tie. "In criminal prosecutions the state has to prove the defendant *intended* to commit the act prohibited by law. It's called *mens rea*. That's Latin for 'guilty mind.' If you lack the required guilty mind, you can't be convicted."

Jessica's sea green eyes widened. *Of course,* she reasoned, *if a person accidentally bumps into me, they're not guilty of assault, are they?* "And since I didn't *know* it was cocaine in that package, they'll have to let me go, right?" Why hadn't she told Mr. Mills about the mysterious man sooner?

Mr. Mills nodded hesitantly. "It's not that simple, I'm afraid. We have to *prove* you didn't know there were drugs in the package. Unfortunately proving a negative is one of the hardest jobs a lawyer has to tackle."

Jessica felt her hopes sink. How were they going to do that? Not even Nick was ready to believe her story about how she'd come to have the cocaine in her possession.

The judge banged his gavel to signal the end of one bail hearing and the beginning of the next. "*The State of California versus Harvey Owens* may now approach the bench," he intoned.

Jessica watched the aisle, expecting a man and his lawyer to make their way toward the judge. No one moved. Jessica could sense a strange, excited buzz take hold of the room.

Suddenly the judge appeared to puff up by six inches. "I said *State of California versus Harvey Owens* approach the bench!" he bellowed. The room immediately silenced, and all eyes scanned the courtroom for the luckless Mr. Owens.

Mr. Mills shook his head and whispered, "Poor guy. Judge Dodd hates being kept waiting. He'll be lucky to make bail at all."

"Judge Dodd!" Jessica gasped. She felt the color drain from her face. *I thought the judge was a kindly old grandfather. But he's the one Marian warned me about. I don't stand a chance!*

"Mr. Owens," Judge Dodd roared. "I'm going to cite you for contempt if you keep my court waiting one second longer! Now where are you?"

"We're here, Your Honor," a man in a brown herringbone suit cried. He ran up to the judge, dragging the terrified Mr. Owens behind him. "I'm sorry, Your Honor," he babbled. "There was a pileup on the freeway."

"I don't care if the world came to an end!" Judge Dodd shouted. "No one, and I mean no one, holds up my courtroom! I'm throwing your case out of here. Take it up with the bailiff for rescheduling, but you'd better pray it's not while I'm at the bench!" He slammed down his gavel and glared at the rest of the room, daring anyone to challenge him. Harvey Owens and his lawyer skulked to the back of the room to talk to the bailiff.

Judge Dodd rapped his gavel again. *"The State of California versus Jessica Wakefield,"* he announced.

Jessica jumped to her feet and would have run to the judge's bench had Mr. Mills not restrained her.

"Calm down," he whispered. "You must be orderly in front of Judge Dodd."

Jessica nodded in terror. She followed Mr. Mills to a table on the judge's right and took a seat.

Judge Dodd peered down at her with barely disguised contempt. "Drug case," she heard him mutter to himself.

Immediately a man in a blue pinstripe suit stood up and approached the judge.

"Who's that?" Jessica asked.

"The district attorney," Mr. Mills replied. "He's the one who'll be prosecuting your case."

Jessica swallowed hard. The district attorney looked sharp in his tailored suit. Certainly sharper than Mr. Mills in his rumpled old clothes.

"Your Honor," the district attorney intoned confidently, "the state has compelling evidence that the defendant possessed cocaine with the intent to sell. She was apprehended by undercover officers and found to be carrying a hundred grams of the drug. The state intends to prosecute and to seek the maximum penalty of twelve to fifteen years in prison."

The district attorney sat down as Jessica's eyes widened into two terrified circles. Twelve to fifteen years! She'd be an old lady by the time she got out.

Mr. Mills jumped to his feet. "Your Honor, the defendant was unaware of the contents of the package in her possession. She didn't intend to distribute drugs. In fact, she lacked the *mens rea* required for even a possession charge. I move that the case be dismissed."

Judge Dodd shook his head. "The state's allegations are very serious, and frankly, Mr. Mills, the evidence is strong." He seemed to think for a minute. "I'm going to convene a special public grand jury hearing over which I plan personally to preside. The grand jury will consider your client's defense and decide whether an indictment should be issued and a full trial held."

Mr. Mills sat down. "That's good news," he told Jessica. "It means we'll have two chances to clear your name. First during the grand jury's indictment hearing. Then, if we need it, during the full trial too."

Full trial! That didn't sound like very good

news. Jessica had been hoping to clear this up today! "But when do I get to go home?" she implored.

"That's next," Mr. Mills whispered to her.

The district attorney again rose and approached the judge's bench. "Your Honor, due to the seriousness of the charges, the state feels that Ms. Wakefield would be a flight risk. We move that she be held without bail at the Sweet Valley county jail until the indictment hearing."

The Sweet Valley county jail! That was where real criminals were sent. Jessica felt tears welling up in her eyes.

Mr. Mills leaped up quickly. "Your Honor," he awkwardly interrupted, "with all due respect, Ms. Wakefield has deep ties within the community. She is a student at SVU, which she attends with her sister and brother. Her parents are from the district. She poses no risk of flight whatsoever. She should be released into the custody of her family on her own recognizance."

Jessica felt Judge Dodd's disdainful gaze fall upon her. He shook his head ruefully. "I can't think of anything loosening the fabric of this society as badly as drugs," he announced. "Drugs are a scourge on our campuses, ruining young lives and robbing our children of their dreams and motivation. There is nothing in this world that I detest more than drugs." He stared pointedly at

Jessica. "Except the people who deal them."

Jessica could barely breathe. This was too horrible! The judge sounded as if he'd already made up his mind that she was guilty. Was he going to refuse her bail?

Judge Dodd looked down at her with a sneer. "Under the circumstances I plan to make an example of you, Miss Wakefield. I order bail to be set at two hundred fifty thousand dollars and that you be remanded to the Sweet Valley county jail until such time as your bail bond is posted."

There was a huge gasp from the audience. Jessica turned to see the color drain out of the faces of Elizabeth, Steven, and Billie. All day no bail had been set anywhere near that high.

"That's a quarter of a million dollars!" Jessica whispered frantically. "Where could I ever get that?"

Mr. Mills slumped in the seat next to her, shaking his head. "He expects any drug dealer to have a lot of ready cash lying around. If you could get together ten percent, a bondsman would put up the rest."

Jessica shook her head, tears coming to her eyes. "I can't. I don't have any money." Even Lila couldn't come up with a sum like that on short notice. Jessica felt a sob escape her throat. "I can't go to jail," she told Mr. Mills frantically.

"I just can't." *Oh, Nick, why are you letting this happen to me?*

"I'm sorry, Jessica," Mr. Mills said, putting a comforting hand on her trembling shoulder. "But you've got to stay strong. There's nothing else we can do right now."

He stood up and approached the bench. "Your Honor, my client will be unable to post bail."

The judge snorted and banged his gavel. "Then I remand her into the custody of the county jailer and order that all parties appear in this courtroom tomorrow morning at precisely nine A.M. for the grand jury indictment hearing."

"Tomorrow morning!" Mr. Mills cried. "Your Honor, we need time to put together a case."

The judge shook his head. "In this state we're tough on drugs," he barked. "And in my courtroom justice is swift!" He turned to Jessica, focusing her with contemptuous eyes. "Is there anything you have to say for yourself before you're sent down?"

Jessica jumped to her feet and turned directly to Nick, tears streaming down her face. "I want everyone to know I would never sell drugs!" she choked. "Please, Nick, please believe me! I didn't do it!"

*   *   *

"Why is everything going so wrong?" Elizabeth moaned to herself as she drove back to campus from the courtroom. "First me and Tom, and now Jessica." She shuddered, remembering the look on her twin's stricken, terrified face as the judge set that impossible bail. "I wish I could change places with her," she cried. "I wouldn't care." With the way Elizabeth felt right now, it wouldn't matter if she were locked up or not.

"Stop it, Liz," she scolded herself. "You and Tom breaking up isn't the end of the world." She took a deep breath and maneuvered the Jeep into a parking spot. *Maybe so,* she thought, *but it sure feels that way.*

Elizabeth began threading her way across campus, barely registering the beautiful, crisp morning with its deep blue sky and bright California sunshine. Up ahead a happy couple walked together arm in arm. Elizabeth's mind was again flooded with thoughts of Tom.

"We made a great team," she whispered, feeling tears threatening to spill down her cheeks. She took a deep breath and swallowed them back. *If Tom and I were still together,* she thought, *we'd be out hunting down evidence to help Jess.* This breakup wasn't only hurting her, it could be hurting her twin as well.

"I know I'm a complete person on my own," Elizabeth told herself. "But being with Tom made everything a little nicer." Now she couldn't control her tears as they ran freely down her cheeks.

Elizabeth walked blindly in the direction of Dickenson Hall, her head bent low. She didn't even notice she'd veered off the path until she ran smack into a hard body. Books and papers went flying everywhere.

"Are you all right?" she gasped, looking up to see a young man flailing his hands to keep from falling. His baseball cap had been knocked sideways, covering his face.

"Liz!" Todd Wilkins exclaimed as he righted his cap.

"Todd," Elizabeth cried back. "Let me help you." She dropped to her knees and started to gather up his books and papers. "I'm so sorry."

Todd ran for a piece of paper that had been caught by the wind and then dropped down next to her. "Whew, I'm fine. But how are you? No broken bones, I hope."

Elizabeth looked up into his familiar, dancing brown eyes and tried to smile.

His face turned immediately serious. "Liz," he said, alarmed. "You've been crying. What's wrong?"

Elizabeth hung her head, wiping the tears from her face with the sleeve of her tailored dress. "Everything," she began, shaking as a fresh sob ran through her body. "Jessica's been arrested."

"You're kidding, Liz," he murmured, taking her arm and pulling her up. He scooped up his books and papers with his other hand and then led her over to an empty bench off the main path that cut across campus. "Sit. Tell me what's going on."

Elizabeth sighed, not knowing if she could face recounting the story. Especially not to someone who was as self-centered as Todd. *But Todd isn't acting that way,* she thought. She looked up at him through her tears. He was smiling at her gently, waiting for her to go on. *He seems like he really cares . . . the way he used to.* Elizabeth felt a warm swelling in her chest. Under his supportive gaze, she felt her strength returning. She quickly filled him in on what was happening with Jessica.

Todd let out a low whistle. "Busted for cocaine. That's a tough one, Liz. Jessica's been in a lot of scrapes over the years, but this one is serious."

Elizabeth nodded sadly and stared dejectedly at the tip of her black pumps. "I know. I've always been there for her, but now I feel help-less."

Todd's smile was warm and reassuring. "I remember. Whatever mess Jessica got herself into, you always managed to get her out of it. You're the best sister she could have."

Elizabeth felt new tears standing in her eyes. "Thanks, Todd. It's hard to feel that way, seeing her behind bars. I wish there were something I could do now."

Todd nodded sympathetically, his soft brown hair rustling a little in the breeze. Elizabeth remembered how she used to run her fingers through it. "I'm sure she knows you're doing your best."

Elizabeth smiled and wondered briefly if Todd's hair was still as soft as it once had been. "You always did know the right things to say." *Like when we were at Sweet Valley High*, Elizabeth thought. She and Todd had been practically inseparable during high school. Todd had been more than Elizabeth's boyfriend; he'd been one of her best friends too. But things had changed when they'd gotten to SVU. Todd had become a Big Man on Campus, with an ego too swelled to let anybody else in. He'd wanted their relationship to become more physically intimate, even though Elizabeth hadn't been ready for such a serious step. They'd broken up, and Todd had become involved with another girl while Elizabeth, after many miserable weeks, had fallen in love with Tom. Now Todd was dating Gin-Yung Suh, a sports reporter for the campus newspaper.

Elizabeth shook her head. Once she'd felt that all Todd's changes had been for the bad, but now he seemed to be changing back. He was more like the old Todd, sensitive, a good listener, and someone she could rely on. Everything Tom wasn't, lately. Elizabeth fought an impulse to rest her head on Todd's broad shoulder. *He might sound and act like the old Todd,* she thought, *but he's not mine anymore.*

"How are *you?*" Elizabeth asked, sitting straighter. "So far we've only talked about me and my problems. You look great."

Todd grinned. "Well, I'm fine, but—" His brown eyes clouded a little and took on a faraway look. He leaned back against the bench.

Elizabeth frowned with concern.

Todd put up his hand. "Don't worry, I'm sure it's nothing." Again the faraway look came over his eyes. "It's Gin-Yung."

Gin-Yung was one of the best students at SVU and was studying abroad for the semester.

"What's the matter?" Elizabeth asked.

Todd took a deep breath and shifted the textbooks on his lap. "Her first couple of letters were fine. Full of all the wonderful things she was seeing and the people she was meeting. She had a lot of work to do, but nothing she couldn't handle."

Elizabeth nodded. That sounded like Gin-Yung.

"But lately," Todd went on, "she writes that some days she has barely enough energy to get out of bed. Her grades are suffering and she's stopped socializing." Todd ran a hand through his wavy hair. "I can't help worrying about it. It's not like her."

"Could it be she's overworked?" Elizabeth suggested, looking up at him. "A new environment. New people. It's bound to be stressful."

Todd nodded. "You're probably right. After all, you should know. You're always working too hard yourself." He gave her a wry smile. "How do you handle the stress?"

Elizabeth managed a small laugh. "I'll let you know when I figure it out."

"Speaking of stress," Todd cried, jumping to his feet. "If I don't get to my ten o'clock class, I'm going to be loaded with it." He quickly gathered his books and then turned to her. "Will you be OK?"

Elizabeth nodded. "Sure. Thanks for talking to me."

Todd cocked his head and smiled. "My pleasure." He bent down and planted a friendly kiss on her cheek. "Call me if you need to talk some more. Anytime."

"Thanks, Todd," Elizabeth said warmly. She watched as he dashed off in the direction of the sociology building. *He really has changed,* she thought. He was understanding and honest with his feelings.

"I bet Todd wouldn't accuse me of lying about his father," she mumbled, starting back to her dorm room. "He would believe in me. Not like Tom."

Police Chief Wallace leaned back in his creaking office chair and laced his meaty fingers behind his head. "Fox, what do you have to say for yourself?"

Nick closed the chief's door and took a seat across the battered desk from him. "This and that," Nick replied, setting his motorcycle helmet on the floor beside him. "This and that." It was how they always started their conversations, a little ritual between detective and boss until they got down to business.

The chief opened the side drawer of his desk and slid out a thin wooden box full of thick, fragrant cigars. He crinkled one between his stubby thumb and forefinger and then held it under his wide, fleshy nose, inhaling deeply. He smiled. "Nothing like a well-deserved stogie. Congratulations, Nick, on a job well done." He offered Nick the opened box.

Whenever a suspect was apprehended by his undercover drug squad, the chief offered the arresting officer a cigar. Nick hesitated.

"No thanks, Chief." As far as Nick was concerned, the case wasn't finished. Jessica's story and the emotional plea she'd made in the courtroom after her bail hearing had convinced him. He knew in his heart they'd arrested the wrong girl.

One of the chief's bushy eyebrow's shot up. "Too early in the day for you, Nick? What am I going to use to motivate you?" He grinned a self-satisfied grin.

Nick shook his head. "I'll have a cigar when this case is *really* closed."

The chief pursed his lips and deftly snipped an eighth of an inch off the end of the cigar with his scissors. "You saying the case isn't closed?" He pushed out his bottom lip. "Now that's interesting." He reached for the stack of folders on the edge of his desk and pulled the top one toward him. He flipped it open. "Says here you've arrested a Ms. Jessica Wakefield." He closed the file and looked at Nick. "She was your contact at SVU, if I recall."

Nick looked out the window over the chief's head to the Sweet Valley courthouse. The clock in the tower showed 11:00 A.M. Jessica would have reached the county jail by now. He sighed. "Wakefield was my cover, not my drug contact. I have strong doubts about her involvement with the coke deal."

Again the chief raised an eyebrow and consulted the file. Nick knew he was only making a show of it. Police Chief Wallace knew every drug case that came through his office inside and out. "Says here," the chief read, "that at seven-thirteen P.M. on Tuesday evening, Jessica Wakefield was apprehended by two plainclothes police detectives and found to be in possession of a hundred grams of high-quality cocaine." He looked up at Nick. "I seem to recall you slapped the handcuffs on her yourself. Sounds to me as if she was caught red-handed."

Nick grimaced. He recognized the words from his report as the chief knew he would. "I know what it says as well as you do, but—"

This time both the chief's eyebrows shot up. "But what?"

Nick gritted his teeth. *Exactly*, he thought. *What?* He didn't have any evidence. He couldn't even be positive of Jessica's innocence. All he had was a gut feeling. The cop's intuition that told him when to push and when to hold back—who was lying and who wasn't. Intuition had saved him more than once when his undercover operations had put his life in danger. He had to trust it now. "I'm not convinced of Ms. Wakefield's guilt."

The chief rolled his eyes and shoved the cigar in his mouth. "Let me tell you how I see it." He took his silver-plated lighter from his pocket and flicked it open, bringing the flame up to the cigar. He puffed at it and then took a long draw. "You go undercover. You meet a pretty young college girl and you let your judgment get clouded. When it turns out that she's involved in drugs, your ego can't take it." The chief blew a smoke ring and poked a finger through it as it hung in the air. "You broke the cardinal rule, Nick. You got involved with your quarry."

"I can't testify against her," Nick blurted, surprising even himself with the finality in his voice.

The chief rolled some ash off his cigar into the ashtray. "The indictment hearing is tomorrow," he stated. "You *will* testify on behalf of this department."

Nick closed his eyes. He'd never put his job on the line for a suspect before. He'd never put *anything* on the line for another person. Nick lived by the code of a cop—stay true to yourself, don't get involved. But then, he'd never met a suspect, or anyone else, like Jessica Wakefield. He opened his eyes and looked directly at the chief. "I can't do it. Not until I'm sure."

The chief shrugged, squinting at Nick through a cloud of smoke. "I'm not *asking*, Detective Fox. I'm *telling* you. Do your job."

Nick shook his head.

The chief sat forward with a bang. "Either agree to be in that courtroom tomorrow morning or else—"

There was no mistaking the menace in the chief's voice. "Or else what?" Nick asked the question quietly, but his heart was pounding and his knuckles were turning white from gripping the sides of the metal chair.

The chief stared at him hard for a moment and then put his cigar into the ashtray. "It's your badge and your gun."

Nick clenched his teeth. *Suspended*, he thought. *Is it worth it? Is it worth losing my job?* But then the vision of Jessica's lovely face, terrified and tear-stained, came back to him, pulling at his heart.

"Suit yourself," he said, snapping open his safety holster and putting his gun on the chief's desk. He pulled his detective's shield out of the pocket of his flannel shirt and dropped it onto the desk as well. Then he stood up and looked directly at the chief. "I'd rather be suspended than send an innocent girl to jail." He reached forward and snapped the cigar sitting in the ashtray in two.

"Get out of here, Fox," the chief growled, sweeping Nick's gun and badge into the top drawer of his desk. "Consider yourself suspended until further notice."

Nick grabbed his helmet and stormed out of the police station on shaky legs. "Nice work, Nick," he told himself as he climbed onto his bike. "You threw your job away for a woman who might be a drug dealer and a world-class liar." He kick-started the big Triumph and shook his head ruefully. He'd put everything on the line for Jessica based on his feelings for her. Now he needed more than just love and faith—he needed hard proof that would either clear her name or seal her fate—and he needed it fast.

Chapter Five

Alex's bright green eyes scanned the substance-abuse hot-line room as she waited for her next phone call. At this early hour the phones were still relatively calm. The people who needed the hot line were just starting to wake up with their hangovers and their feelings of dread about the "night before."

Alex smiled faintly to herself as she took in the shabby but comfortable chairs, the malfunctioning coffee machine with the chipped coffee mugs, and the brightly colored posters: One day at a time. Easy does it. Think before you drink.

It was from a hot-line room like this that the wonderful T-Squared, aka Noah Pearson, Alex's boyfriend, had helped her get sober.

"Luckily he's still putting up with me!" Alex

exclaimed, thinking of their most recent fight.

Suddenly her console started blinking like a Christmas tree. Alex glanced at her Swatch. Eleven A.M., right on time. The natives were waking up.

Alex pushed in the first button. "Substance-abuse hot line," she answered.

"I'm in so much trouble," a shaky voice cried.

Alex gripped the phone tightly. She recognized the voice immediately. It was the guy who'd called two days ago, frantic that his girlfriend might be mixing him up in a drug deal that he didn't have the willpower to resist. "It's OK," Alex said. "Calm down. Tell me what happened." Her own heart raced as if she were running a marathon.

She heard a choked sob in the background.

"Are you there?" *Oh, please, don't hang up,* she thought. "Are you all right? You and I spoke the other day, didn't we? About your girlfriend?"

"Yes," he croaked.

Alex could hear him expel a deep breath.

"I was right. It was drugs."

Alex felt an excited chill raise goose bumps on her bare arms. *Could this have anything to do with Jessica?* she wondered, her mind racing. Everyone at Theta house had heard that Jessica was in jail for cocaine possession.

"I had to show up at this meeting and hand over a package." The caller was being awfully cagey, but Alex checked herself against pushing him. After all, she was there to help people, not grill them for information. "I swear I didn't know for sure there were drugs in the package. She set me up. My girlfriend set me up!"

"It's OK," Alex soothed. "Talk it out."

The guy on the other end sniffled and then continued, his voice cracking after each word. "I handed off the package and was given a big hatbox in return."

"A hatbox?" Alex blurted. She mentally kicked herself for slipping out of professional mode.

The man breathed hard. "Yes, with a big, floppy white hat in it."

Alex frowned. That didn't sound like much of a drug deal.

As if reading her mind, he continued. "I was supposed to get money, and now my girlfriend said if I don't come up with the cash, she's going to turn me over to the mobsters who gave her the drugs. They'll kill me! I don't know what to do!"

Alex gasped. She'd been taught to counsel kids with drug and alcohol cravings . . . to resist the urges on a one-day-at-a-time basis. She didn't know how to help someone escape from killers. "Have you talked to the police?"

"I can't," the guy cried. "My girlfriend said they'll put me in jail!"

"But what's your alternative?" Alex asked, her knees shaking. "It's better than being killed."

"I'm running away," he stated firmly, then choked back a sob. "My girlfriend doesn't know where I'm from. She never cared about my history. She never cared about me at all. She used me."

"It's OK," Alex said reassuringly. "I care about you. Running away isn't going to help."

"Where I'm going, no one will find me. My family lives in a small town along the coast. I'll be safe there. Wish me luck."

"Wait!" Alex screamed into the phone. There was silence on the other end. She kept the phone to her ear, willing the man to come back on the line. But then the silence was broken by the recorded voice of an operator reminding her to hang up the phone. He was gone.

"Tom, son," Mr. Conroy's friendly voice boomed as he flung open the front door of his modern Los Angeles condo. "Come in. Jake, Mary, your big brother is here."

Tom's spunky half brother and half sister came racing down the hallway in their pajamas and wrapped their arms around his legs.

"Easy." Mr. Conroy chuckled, pulling the

kids away. "Let your brother breathe." He rolled his eyes good-naturedly and led Tom down into the sunken living room, where a leather sofa and two plush cream-colored chairs were arranged around a big wooden coffee table. "Where's the lovely Elizabeth?" he asked. "I thought she'd be with you."

Tom took a seat across from his father. "I didn't invite her."

"Oh?" his father inquired, tugging the knees of his slacks and leaning forward on the sofa. "I got the impression the two of you went everywhere together. Never seen a couple more in love."

Tom studied the selection of magazines on the coffee table, steeling himself for what was to come. He had to ask his father about Elizabeth's allegations. Even though Tom knew her story was pure fantasy, after his run-in with Danny last night he'd started to feel uneasy. He owed it to his father to dispel any lingering doubts.

Mary skipped over and perched on the arm of Mr. Conroy's sofa. "Who's Elizabeth?"

"Tom's girlfriend, honey," Mr. Conroy told her. "She has pretty blond hair like yours. Only hers is combed back into a ponytail." He tickled Mary's side, causing her to squirm with laughter. "Why don't you go put your hair back too?"

"OK," she squealed, running off down the hall.

"*Former* girlfriend," Tom mumbled, feeling his anxiety level rising. How could he bring up Elizabeth's accusations without upsetting his father? *What if Dad thinks I'm accusing him?* He'd have every right to throw Tom out of his house. *And out of his life,* Tom thought.

Jake walked up to Tom's chair, tossing a softball up in the air. "Can we play ball now?"

Mr. Conroy crossed his arms in mock sternness. "In your pajamas? Why don't you get dressed and then we'll go to the park."

Jake threw the ball up once more as if weighing his options and then ran off after his sister.

Mr. Conroy ran a hand through his thinning brown hair. "These school holidays—" He sighed and then turned his attention back to Tom. "You were saying something about Liz?"

Tom looked away for a moment and gritted his teeth. He had to get this over with sooner or later. "Elizabeth and I have broken up."

"Oh, son," Mr. Conroy said sadly. "I'm sorry to hear that. Is there anything I can do? Talk to her, maybe?" He ran his fingers through his hair again. "I could have the two of you over for dinner this weekend. Maybe a night in L.A. would help patch things up?"

Tom looked up at his father, shaking his head. "Thanks, Dad, but I don't think that would do much good."

Mr. Conroy frowned. "Don't think that way." He shifted in his seat on the sofa across from Tom. "Lovers' tiffs are always hard, but rarely unmendable. I'm sure if two smart guys like us put our heads together, we can get you and Liz back together."

If only Elizabeth could hear my father now, Tom thought bitterly. *He really cares about her, cares about us as a couple.*

"So what's this all about?" Mr. Conroy asked. "Did you forget a special anniversary or something?"

Tom smiled weakly. *If only it were that easy,* he thought.

Tom screwed up his courage and then blurted out the truth. "I broke up with Liz because she made some wild accusations about you."

"Me?" Mr. Conroy sat back, a look of shock on his face. "What kind of accusations? I hope she didn't think I was an interfering father for tracking you down. I certainly don't want to intrude on your life if I'm not wanted."

"No, no," Tom assured him. "I couldn't be happier. Liz knows that. That's why her accusations are all the worse."

"What did she say?" Mr. Conroy asked, his face still white and shaken. "Tell me. There shouldn't be any secrets between a father and his son."

Tom hesitated. *Please don't let this hurt my relationship with my father,* he prayed. He raised his eyes to meet Mr. Conroy's head-on. "Liz says you've been making unwanted sexual advances toward her. I know it can't possibly be true, Dad, but I need to hear it from you. Have you been putting the moves on Elizabeth?"

"Celine, you've outdone yourself," Gloria Abel and Kimberly Schyler gushed in unison, surrounding her with delighted squeals. "Our Theta parlor is sensational!" The official parlor opening ceremony had just ended with Celine cutting a baby blue ribbon across the doorway. Now about twenty of her new Theta sisters were milling around, examining the new decor.

Celine smiled sweetly and selected a shrimp from the tray of tastefully prepared seafood on the coffee table. "Yes, the room is marvelous, isn't it?" She reclined against one of the plush turquoise velvet sofas and surveyed the newly redecorated parlor. Her parlor. Her sofa, her chairs, her drapes, and her thick double-piled carpet, all in varying shades of blue and green. *At least until the credit card company comes and repossesses it all.* She winced.

"And I love this color scheme!" Tina Chai enthused, dropping down next to Celine and fingering the soft material of the sofa. "It goes perfectly with your eyes."

Celine lowered her long, dark eyelashes. "Thank you, ladies," she demurred. "You're too kind." Everyone knew the Boudreaux women looked best in cool colors. Celine's top priority during the redecoration of the parlor had been making sure she looked gorgeous sitting in it. *Now if I can just live long enough to enjoy it,* she thought, an icy stab of fear causing her teeth to chatter.

"Are you cold?" Tina asked

Celine bit her lip and tried to smile. *Why can't I keep these awful thoughts away?* she thought, miffed. *At least long enough so I can enjoy my party.*

"Well, I don't believe Jessica would have anything to do with drugs," came a high voice from the far corner of the parlor.

Celine started. "What's that about Jessica?" she called.

"Didn't you hear?" Tina cried. "She was busted for dealing cocaine. I thought everyone at Theta house knew about it."

Celine's pretty mouth dropped open. "You don't say . . . ," she murmured, her mind racing frantically. Was it possible?

"It's true," Kimberly cut in breathlessly. "She was arrested near the science building last night."

Celine hoped the look of surprise on her face wasn't too obvious. She had no idea how it happened, but that idiot Jordan must have somehow given the package to Jessica! "My, my," she whispered to herself. "So that's why Little Miss Wakefield isn't at my party. I thought she and that Lila Fowler creature were simply boycotting." She ran her tongue along her lips and then reached for another shrimp. "How did that happen?" she asked more loudly.

Tina's hands fluttered excitedly. "Her boyfriend, Nick, turned out to be an undercover cop. *He* arrested her. Isn't it too awful!"

Nick? Celine thought, blanching, her heart pounding in her chest. *That could have been me!* "But it wasn't me," she whispered. "It was Jessica Wakefield." She felt the beginning of a very large smile forming on her lips. Things were certainly looking up. She might be out a lot of money, but the idea of Little Miss Prom Queen sitting behind bars almost made up for it. *Almost,* Celine thought, grimacing. *I still have to keep from ending up as plant fertilizer!*

"Excuse me," a voice called out. "Attention, everyone." It was Denise Waters. The room grew quiet.

"As fellow Thetas," Denise announced, "I expect everyone to show their support for our sister Jessica Wakefield during the difficult indictment hearing and possible trial ahead."

Celine looked at Denise with barely concealed distaste. "Denise needs a redecoration more than this parlor did," Celine muttered to herself. How could Celine be expected to take anyone seriously who wore a T-shirt and jeans to a tea party?

Celine looked down at her own stunning outfit—a gorgeous blue-and-white polka-dot halter dress. She'd spent over an hour and a half on her hair and makeup, plus she'd put on a double dose of her special gardenia perfume. But the *pièce de résistance* was her new floppy white hat, with its exquisite lace trim, that not only made her look beautiful but mysterious as well. A little compensation for that stupid drug deal.

"But surely the authorities wouldn't put Jessica in jail if she wasn't guilty, would they?" Celine called out sweetly, barely suppressing a giggle.

"Are you doubting Jessica's innocence?" an angry voice demanded. The whole room seemed to go quiet.

Celine turned sharply, looking into the flashing gray eyes of Isabella Ricci. "Isabella," she drawled in her thickest, syrup-sweet voice. "Now why should I do that?"

Isabella raised one perfect eyebrow a fraction

of an inch and tossed back her silky black hair. "Because you've always had a problem with the Wakefield twins."

Celine fluttered her eyelashes and stifled a laugh. *Saying I have a problem with the Wakefields,* she thought, *is like saying that Southerners and Yankees don't get along—a gross understatement.*

"I don't have any problem with the Wakefield twins," she announced. "Like all the Thetas, I hope Jessica can overcome her drug problem and come back to us soon. I'll be in the courtroom with the rest of you." *That's for sure,* Celine thought, a shiver of delight passing through her. She wouldn't miss Jessica's undoing for anything in the world.

"This is the final insult," Denise Waters whispered to Alex. "A party to celebrate Celine Boudreaux's decorating taste is an affront to every good sorority sister."

"I'll say," Alex whispered back. As far as she was concerned, the parlor decor was a horror show. All that blue and green was enough to make her seasick.

"And the timing couldn't be worse," Denise continued. "With poor Jessica in jail right now, the last thing I feel like doing is celebrating."

"Really," Alex agreed, checking her watch. Ten more minutes and she was out of there to meet Noah at the cafeteria. As it was, she could barely concentrate on what the other girls were saying. Her mind was full of thoughts of the mysterious hot-line caller. *If only I could tell Noah*, she thought. *He'd know what to do*. But how could she without breaking the confidentiality of the hot line?

Suddenly Tina Chai and Kimberly Schyler began laughing uproariously at something Celine had said. Alex rolled her eyes, turning her attention back to Denise. "How can they fawn over her like that?" she said with a groan.

She shot a look over at Celine, who was smiling approvingly at her newfound admirers. Celine was overdressed as usual, but Alex had to admit that her floppy white hat was gorgeous. Not at all Celine's usual style.

"And don't think Celine isn't lapping it up like a newborn kitten," Denise remarked. "I can see the milk mustache from here."

Alex grinned. "What I really don't get is how they can stand her awful perfume." She wrinkled her nose. "Celine is the first person I've met who could make the smell of gardenia actually offensive."

Just then Alex spied Lila Fowler coming in the doorway, immaculately attired in a tailored emerald green suit.

"Uh-oh," Denise said, also noticing Lila's

entrance. "Wait until Lila sees Celine's decor. This room is everything her sophisticated taste isn't."

Alex watched the look of disbelief spread across Lila's face as she took in the room.

Denise bit her lip. "Lila's going to have a fit," she said with a giggle.

Alex was about to start laughing too until she saw Lila's disbelief turn into fury. "What's up with Lila?" she asked as she watched Lila storm across the room to where Celine was holding court.

"Where did you get that?" Lila demanded loudly, pointing an accusatory finger at Celine.

The room seemed to go quiet, and Alex moved closer to see what the problem was. Celine tossed a last bite of shrimp into her mouth and pointed to the empty catering tray before her. "Don't worry, Lila. I'm sure there are more in the kitchen—"

Alex watched as Lila's large blue eyes narrowed, her full red lips pulled back in a snarl. "I meant the hat."

"Oh, this." Celine tinkled with laughter. She took off the hat and fingered the material. "Lovely, isn't it?"

A few of the girls murmured in agreement.

"What's going on?" Denise whispered furiously in Alex's ear.

"I don't know," Alex whispered back. "Something to do with Celine's hat."

Lila crossed her arms, her cheeks flushed. "Yes, it's quite unique," she said, each word enunciated carefully. "You must tell me where you got it."

Celine positioned the hat back on her head. "I couldn't say, Lila. This hat has been in the Boudreaux family for ages."

Lila said nothing, but Alex could see that her friend was fuming. Smoke was practically curling out of her ears.

"We'll see about that," Lila muttered, turning. She headed toward Alex and Denise as the other conversations around the room started up again.

"What's up, Lila?" Alex asked. She glanced at her watch again. Noah would be arriving at the cafeteria any minute. But she had to find out what was eating her friend. "I thought you were going to rip that hat right off Celine's evil little head."

Lila took her and Denise's arms and pulled them into a corner. "That hat looks like the one I had custom-made at Sweet Valley Milliners," Lila sputtered angrily. "I think Celine must have gone and bought it out from under my nose."

"Ouch." Denise grimaced. "But why would the milliners do that?"

"Maybe they were confused," Lila theorized. "I called them the other day to tell them that a friend would be coming by for the hat. Jessica had promised to pick it up for me, but obviously she never got the chance."

"Jessica was picking up your hat?" Alex croaked excitedly. Suddenly her mind was racing. Hadn't the hot-line caller told her he'd gotten a hat in exchange for the drugs?

"Yes, why?" Lila looked at her curiously.

"Oh, just asking," Alex replied breathlessly. All she knew was she had to find Noah—had to figure out what to do. And *fast*.

Tom watched as Mr. Conroy's mouth dropped almost to his chest. He banged his ear with the palm of his hand. "I'm sorry, Tom. I must be having trouble with my hearing." He gave a little laugh. "Liz accused *me* of coming on to her?"

Tom nodded solemnly.

Mr. Conroy shook his head in disbelief and looked Tom squarely in the eye. "That's completely untrue, son. I hope you know that I would never do anything to come between you and Elizabeth."

Tom watched in horror as his father's jaw began to wobble. Tears came to the older man's eyes. "This is all my fault. It was selfish of me to crash into your life after all this time. If I'd never turned up, you wouldn't be having this trouble. You and Liz would still be together."

His father looked so upset and stricken that Tom felt tears coming to his own eyes. "Dad, no," he tried to reassure him. This was his worst nightmare. His father was now regretting having contacted Tom at all.

Mr. Conroy continued, his mouth turned down and his shoulders slumped. "I gave you up once and I guess I'll have to suffer for the rest of my life. I had some nerve, thinking I could be forgiven after all this time." Mr. Conroy grimaced. "Though Liz was the last person I thought would resent me enough to make up a story like that. Son, I'm sorry. I'll clear out of your life right now if you want."

"No, Dad," Tom cried loudly, jumping up. There was no way he'd let another family be ripped away from him. He'd do anything to prevent that. "I know Liz's story is a pack of lies. It's not your fault."

Mr. Conroy's face darkened slightly and he pinched his bottom lip between his fingers. "No, Tom, I've caused you enough heartache already. I'll let you alone."

"Dad, please," Tom pleaded, twisting his hands while he stood over his father. "I never believed her for a minute. I know you wouldn't do something like that. It was Liz who betrayed me, not you. I'm glad she pulled this stunt before I got any more deeply involved with her. I know the kind of person she is now."

Mr. Conroy sniffed back a tear. "Are you sure? Because I don't want any misunderstandings coming between us."

"Of course, Dad," Tom smiled encouragingly. He bent down and gave the older man a big hug. "You're my dad and you're back in my life. That's all that matters to me. That's all that will ever matter."

Chapter Six

"Noah!" Alex waved frantically, seeing the shaggy blond head of her good-looking boyfriend at one of the crowded tables in the SVU cafeteria. Noah motioned to an empty seat beside him.

Alex wove her way across the noisy room and collapsed into a chair. She'd run all the way from Theta house, practically bursting with dark suspicions about Celine and the hat that Lila claimed was hers. *But the hat is meaningless without the information the caller gave me*, she thought with frustration. *And I can't tell Noah about the call.*

She stared into Noah's big brown eyes, practically willing him to ask her what was going on.

"What is it?" he asked, slightly alarmed. "I haven't gotten this much scrutiny since I broke out with chicken pox."

"Noah," she began. "When you were on the hot line, did you ever break a confidence?"

Noah put down his sandwich and gave her a level gaze. "Why? Is someone in trouble?"

Alex nodded. "Yes, and I don't know what to do about it."

Noah sighed. "There were times when I wanted to. I once had a girl who talked about hurting herself. But she told me she was terrified of people finding out. She said if I told anyone, she'd never call again. So I didn't."

"Did it turn out all right?"

Noah nodded. "In the end. I convinced her to go see someone, but those first couple of nights I didn't sleep."

Alex picked up a paper napkin and began unconsciously shredding it.

Noah put his hand over hers. "Did someone threaten suicide?"

Alex shook her head. She opened her mouth to speak and then closed it again.

"Alex," Noah said softly, "maybe if you tell me a little, in a general way, I could help."

Alex swallowed hard. *After all*, she thought, *Noah has worked on a hot line. If we discuss a call, that's not idle gossip. It's two colleagues discussing a difficult case*. And she had to do something. It was tearing her apart.

"Noah, can I tell you *specifically* what happened?" If he was willing to listen, she would tell him.

He studied her face. For a moment she was afraid he was going to refuse, tell her he'd only listen if the story was vague, but something in her eyes must have convinced him otherwise. "OK." He nodded.

Alex quickly filled him in on everything she'd learned from the hot-line caller. "Don't you see, Noah? It must have been the same drug deal. It's too much of a coincidence otherwise." Alex paused for breath and then went on. "A guy being twisted around his girlfriend's little finger makes a drug deal and gets a hat in return. Then today Celine shows up at the Theta party wearing a floppy white hat that Lila says Jessica was supposed to pick up for her."

"Whoa!" Noah said, holding up his hand. "Now you're losing me. What does Celine have to do with it?"

Alex gripped Noah's arm. "If Jessica picked up Lila's hat," she said excitedly, "and somehow gave it to the hot-line caller, then Celine must be involved. How else could she have gotten hold of Lila's hat?"

Noah nodded, realization slowly dawning on his handsome face. "*If* Jessica picked up the hat, then you might be on to something about Celine." He thought for a minute. "But regardless, we've got to go to the police. The information from the hot-line caller alone could be critical to Jessica's case."

Alex cringed. "But you said that you didn't call the police even when you thought a girl was going to attempt suicide."

Noah pushed his plate to one side and drummed his fingers on the cafeteria table. Alex could imagine the cogs turning in his brain, deliberating, working out a solution. Finally he sat forward and took her hand.

"This is different, Alex. Your caller was an unwitting accomplice to a serious crime. You'd be thwarting a police investigation if you didn't report it. And anyway, it's not like you're giving the guy up. You don't even know who he is. You're just giving the police something to think about and hopefully help them clear Jessica's name."

Alex squeezed his hand and smiled. They both knew it was far-fetched, but Noah had come up with a good argument to assuage her guilt. "So you think it will help?"

"If we get the information to the right cops. It would be a mistake if we reported it in a general way. We need to approach the person directly involved in Jessica's case."

"Nick Fox," Alex cried.

Noah did a double take. "Nick Fox is a cop?"

"Undercover." Alex nodded. "He arrested Jessica."

"The poor guy." Noah shook his head in amazement. "I heard he and Jessica were pretty serious. Sure looked that way."

Alex's eyes widened. She hadn't even thought about what Nick must be going through. "We've got to tell him. I'm sure he's dying for a lead to help Jessica."

Elizabeth looked up from her bed as a sharp rap on the door punctured the stillness of her dorm room.

"Come in," she called, putting a well-worn copy of Jane Austen's *Emma* aside and swinging her feet to the ground. She felt surprise and anger cause her cheeks to flush as her visitor entered. She'd been expecting her best friend, Nina Harper, to drop by after lunch or maybe one of the Thetas coming over to show their support for Jessica. Not Nick Fox!

Nick took a step into the room. His eyes looked haunted. His handsome, chiseled face needed a shave, and his hair was a tangled, windblown mess. "I'm here about Jessica."

Elizabeth leaped to her feet to block him. "Do you have a search warrant?" she demanded. "Because I'm not going to help you convict my sister."

Nick shook his head. "Can I come in?"

Elizabeth angrily crossed her arms. "Why? Your case isn't strong enough, so you're here to plant evidence?" Her bottom lip began to tremble. "Because that's the only way anyone who knows Jessica would ever believe she had anything to do with drugs!"

Nick held up the palms of his hands in surrender. "Look, give me a break. I want evidence, all right, but not to convict Jessica. I'm trying to clear her."

"Oh, sure," Elizabeth spat, tossing back her long blond ponytail and glaring at him. "You got her into this trouble in the first place. If you're having second thoughts, why don't you go tell the authorities you messed up so they'll let her go?"

Nick sighed. "Can I *please* come in? We're attracting a crowd."

Elizabeth looked past him and gasped. Half of Dickenson was standing in the hallway, gaping at them. She took a deep breath and then stepped back from the door, allowing him to enter. "There." She pointed to the least comfortable chair in her dorm room. "You can sit there."

Nick thanked her and grabbed the hardwood chair, flipping it around and straddling it so its back protected the front of his body.

Elizabeth smiled inwardly for a moment, realizing that he sensed her intense anger and might actually be scared of her. She decided to lighten up a fraction. "So what do you want?" she asked in a slightly calmer tone.

Nick rested his chin on the back of the chair. "All the evidence points to your sister's guilt."

"But—" Elizabeth's anger started to flare again.

Nick raised a hand. "I no longer believe it, Elizabeth. But I don't know what to think. She was arrested during a stakeout and she had the drugs in her hands."

"Nick," Elizabeth said. "No one's disputing that. But she didn't know there were drugs in the package."

Nick hunched up his shoulders and looked helplessly around him. "How can I prove it?"

Elizabeth sat down on her bed across from him. "All I can say is that she was dying to find out about you. She showed up where she knew you were supposed to be and intercepted the package meant for you."

Nick gripped the sides of the chair and lifted himself up. "That's what she said, but none of the police officers present saw anyone give her the package. Right now everyone thinks she was the dealer."

Elizabeth punched the mattress. "But you

know that can't be true," she exploded. "Jessica doesn't do drugs. And she certainly wouldn't be involved in selling them."

She grabbed her pillow and squeezed it. *Why is everyone being so blind?* She looked over at Nick, registering in her mind his gorgeous, bad-boy looks. *He's Jessica's type, all right,* she thought. There was even a vague resemblance to Mike McAllery, Jessica's ex-husband.

Elizabeth threw her pillow to the side. "But she *would* follow around a guy she liked and do any crazy thing she could think of to get to know him."

Nick walked over to the window and looked out. His fingers were curled into fists by his sides. "I believe you," he said, his voice suddenly gruff. Gruff in a way that Elizabeth could almost imagine was tinged with emotion. He gulped back air and continued. "Can you think of anything, any hard evidence that could help her case?"

Elizabeth looked over at his strong back, now slumped, his head bent, and realized for the first time that this guy, with his tough looks and his rough manner, was hurting. He really did care about Jessica. *And that means I can trust him to help her. But how?* Elizabeth realized with a start. *If the arresting officer can't clear up this mess, what chance does Jessica have?*

"You want Detective Fox?" the desk sergeant barked. "One flight up. Third door on the left."

"Thank you," Alex said. She and Noah turned away from the front desk and headed toward the staircase at the back of the Sweet Valley Police headquarters. The station was buzzing with activity, full of angry voices and scary-looking criminals, their tattooed arms restrained with handcuffs. Policemen were shouting orders and civilians were rushing around looking for help.

Suddenly two women in short spandex dresses burst out screaming and lunged at each other. "I'm gonna kill you!" one shrieked as she grab a handful of the other woman's hair. Alex jumped out of the way as a sharpened red fingernail sliced past her face. Two burly policewomen jumped in and pulled the women apart.

"Whew," Alex gasped, her heart slamming against her chest. *I was almost sliced to ribbons,* she thought. "I hope Jessica is holding up all right in this madhouse." The lingering doubts she'd had about coming forward and breaking the confidentiality of the hot line were fading fast. There was no way Jessica belonged in this zoo. No matter what prank had gotten her tangled up in a drug deal, Jessica was not a criminal.

Noah nodded vigorously, his eyes wide and nervous.

They followed the desk sergeant's instructions and found themselves outside Police Chief Wallace's office.

"Enter," a husky voice yelled when they knocked.

Alex and Noah stepped in and stood awkwardly before him. "We're looking for Detective Nick Fox," Alex told him.

The police chief tilted back in his chair, linking his fingers behind his head. "What for?"

Alex hesitated and looked over at Noah. They'd agreed to tell Nick about the hot-line caller and the possible connection with Jessica. But that was because Nick was involved. Their decision hadn't included the rest of the police force.

"It's personal," Noah piped up, as if reading Alex's thoughts.

"Personal," the chief said, as if mulling over the word. He righted his chair and studied his fingernail. "So then it's not police business?"

Alex gulped. "Not exactly. At least we're not sure. But we'd really like to talk to Nick."

The chief shrugged and reached for a folder on his desk. Without looking at them, he said, "Sorry, can't help you, then. Nick Fox no longer works for the Sweet Valley Police."

"Where was he transferred?" Noah asked.

"Transferred?" the chief retorted, looking back at them with an enigmatic smile. "I wouldn't know."

What's with him? Alex thought, shuffling her feet. It wasn't even clear whether Nick had left the police force altogether or had just moved to another town. "Well, do you know how we can reach him?" she asked. "A home address or something?"

The chief shook his head. "Sorry, we're not allowed to release police officers'—even former police officers'—home addresses."

"Come on, Alex," Noah mumbled, taking her arm. "Thanks."

For nothing, Alex added in her mind as they closed the office door behind them.

"What was that all about?" Alex asked as they walked down the corridor.

Noah shook his head. "I have no idea. But it sounds like your friend Nick left on bad terms."

"Great." Alex groaned, following Noah out to the parking lot. "Now that we've finally squared it with ourselves to give Nick the information, we can't find him. What should we do?"

Noah unlocked her door and held it open for her. "I don't know." He grimaced. "I hope this isn't a lost cause."

Alex stepped into the car and pulled the door shut. *It can't be,* she thought. *Nick wouldn't have vanished.* She'd seen the way his face lit up around Jessica. He couldn't disappear now that Jessica needed him, could he?

Elizabeth stood uncomfortably in the long, dim visiting room of the Sweet Valley county jail. The visiting area consisted of a pockmarked metal table with chairs bolted on either side. Pairs of people sat whispering to each other across the table's pitted surface.

Elizabeth turned away and stared up at the thin strip of windows that practically hugged the ceiling. They were covered with grime and laced with thick wire mesh that the afternoon sunlight was barely able to penetrate. *Impossible to reach,* she thought. *To prevent escapes.* But even if a prisoner could make it out the window, she or he would still have to scale the seven-foot perimeter fence topped with barbed wire that Elizabeth had seen on the way in. And outmaneuver all those guards and police dogs roaming the yard.

Elizabeth shuddered and wrapped her arms around her white silk blouse. This place was a lot scarier than the Sweet Valley police station. *And this is just the county jail,* she thought. *If Jess is convicted, she'll be sent upstate. And that jail will make this one look like a country club.*

"Liz."

Elizabeth turned as she heard Jessica call her name in a feeble voice. *Oh no*, Elizabeth thought, stifling a gasp. She willed her pretty features into a neutral mask as the matron roughly brought Jessica to a stop. Her sister stood before her in a garish orange jumpsuit with the word *prisoner* stamped across the front in large black letters.

Jessica's face was scrubbed clean of makeup and her eyes were puffy and red from crying. Her long blond hair was yanked back in a tight ponytail and she looked as if she were about to collapse. Elizabeth swallowed a cry. Jessica had only been in custody for two days. In another two weeks her sister's vivacious, beautiful face would be barely recognizable.

"Jess," Elizabeth whispered, putting her hand out for her sister. "Are you OK?"

Jessica took a faltering step toward her. But before she could get any farther, the matron shouted, "Stop! No contact between prisoners and visitors or I'll put you behind the Plexiglas!"

Jessica jumped back as if she'd been burned. Elizabeth felt her heart wrench. *How much more of this can Jess take?*

The matron pointed to two of the chairs

along the table. "Sit there," she ordered. "No touching. No cursing. No exchanging of packages. No raised voices. If you have any objections or break any of these rules, this session will end immediately. If you don't like it, you can take it up with the warden."

Elizabeth watched as Jessica sank down into her chair and crossed her arms. Elizabeth did the same, quickly realizing it was a safeguard to keep them from reaching out to each other.

The matron took up her post in a seat a short distance behind Jessica.

"What's going on, Liz?" Jessica asked in a whisper.

Elizabeth leaned forward a little, keeping her arms pinned. "I talked to Nick. He came by our room."

"Nick?" Jessica asked, her voice rising. "Did you tell him I was innocent? Did you tell him I would never have anything to do with drugs?"

"Shhh . . ." Elizabeth motioned with her head to the matron, who was staring malevolently at them.

Jessica exhaled deeply and slumped her shoulders. "What did he want?" she whispered, her voice back in control.

Elizabeth sat forward a microinch more. "He wants to believe in you. He wants to help. He came by to see if I had any evidence on your behalf."

"Really?" Jessica asked, her voice low but excited. "Does that mean he's going to get me out of here soon?"

Elizabeth shrugged helplessly and gnawed on her bottom lip. "He can't do it by himself, Jess. He needs evidence. It's got to come from you." She shifted slightly in her seat. "Think. Try and remember exactly what happened when you got to the science building."

Jessica scrunched up her pale face. Elizabeth could see how hard she was trying. She wished she could do it for her. But it was Jessica who held the answers.

Jessica sighed. "It's mostly a blur. I was really nervous. I can remember my heart was pounding so hard, I thought it would burst. I kept thinking, 'It's OK, I'm going to find out about Nick, I can do this.' I barely noticed what was going on."

"OK," Elizabeth stated. She'd have to try another tact. She was an investigative reporter. She'd use the same skills she used when going after a story. It was all about the questions you asked. The right ones would trigger Jessica's memory. "What time did you get there?"

Jessica placed her palms on the table. "Around seven."

"Was the guy already there?"

Jessica nodded. "Yes."

Elizabeth adopted a casual tone. "How do you know he was a guy?"

Jessica frowned. "Because . . . he had a deep voice. And he was tall. Tall and skinny."

Elizabeth shrugged. "Maia Stillwater has a deep voice, but no one would think she was a guy."

Jessica's eyes narrowed. "Are you saying I'm wrong about him being a guy?"

Elizabeth looked around the room nonchalantly, acting as if she didn't really care. She was using a ploy that had helped her before in jogging a witness's memory. She hoped it would work this time as well. "No, I was only wondering what makes you so sure. His face?"

Jessica's eyes got a faraway look, as if she were trying to picture the man's face in her mind. "No." She shook her head. "He was wearing a baseball cap pulled down low. I couldn't see his face clearly."

"But you knew it was a guy?" Elizabeth prompted.

"Yes!" Jessica exploded, sounding exasperated. She gave Elizabeth a look as if to say, Why are you driving me crazy? "I could tell he was a guy because—"

"He had a guy's body?" Elizabeth filled in. "And he wasn't wearing a dress?"

Jessica rolled her eyes. "No, he wasn't wear-

ing a dress. He had on a sweatshirt and—"
Jessica gasped and nearly rose from her seat. "A
sweatshirt that said *SVU Engineering* in big letters across the front." A hopeful smile lit up her
face. "Liz, you're a genius."

Elizabeth let out a large stream of pent-up,
anxious breath. "It's a good thing you remembered something. I was afraid you were going
to throttle me."

Jessica let out a little laugh, and Elizabeth
could see the old Jessica peeking out from behind her eyes.

Elizabeth smiled back. "Now we've got
something to work on. How many tall, skinny
SVU engineering students can there be?"

Jessica's smile faded. "Lots," she grumbled.
"Remember when I signed up for the wrong
class and ended up in Engineering 101? They all
looked like that. I think it's a prerequisite."

Elizabeth made a face. "Maybe so, but at
least it narrows the search to a particular department at SVU. It's a lot more to go on than
when we started."

Jessica nodded, her aquamarine eyes brightening slightly.

The matron got up from her chair noisily.
"Time's up," she barked.

Elizabeth and Jessica stood too, keeping a
safe distance from each other.

"It's going to be OK, Jess," Elizabeth assured her with a lot more hope than she actually felt. "This could be our big break."

Jessica gave her a wan smile. "Thanks, Liz. I love you."

"I love you too, Jess," Elizabeth called, blinking back tears as Jessica was led away. "I'll get this information to Nick. Don't you worry. We'll get you out of here. I promise."

"If it's the last thing I do," Elizabeth added to herself. "I'll get you out of here."

Chapter
Seven

_____

"Hey, Beauty Queen, chow time."

Jessica looked up from her cot in the county jail and gasped. Two hardened women were leaning on either side of the entrance to her cell. Moments before all the doors had mechanically opened and a loud bell had rung, signaling dinnertime.

Jessica slowly swung her feet to the cement floor. "Thanks," she said nervously. "What's on the menu?"

The smaller of the two women snorted. "Did you get a load of that, Rerun?" she addressed the bigger one.

Rerun chortled and mimicked Jessica with cruel accuracy. "What's on the menu?"

Jessica grimaced. These two were in black jumpsuits with _prisoner_ printed in orange. She tried another stab at civility. "Why are your uniforms different from mine?"

"Duh, because we've been here longer?" The smaller woman sneered.

"Why are your uniforms different from mine?" Rerun parroted spitefully.

Jessica could see a glint of malice in their mocking eyes. She quickly looked around her tiny cell. But other than the cot she'd just vacated and a sink in the corner there was nothing else. There was no place to run and nowhere to hide. Her only way out was past the two women blocking the cell door. "What do you want?" she croaked.

Rerun started to echo her again. "What do—" Rerun cut off in midsentence as the smaller woman held up her hand. *So she's the boss,* Jessica thought frantically, turning her full attention to her. *And Rerun is the muscle.*

"We want to teach you some rules," the boss informed her contemptuously. "Like, you don't ask questions. We do. If I say 'jump,' you say 'how high?'"

Jessica's heart thudded wildly in her chest. What would they do if she didn't?

"Now jump, Beauty Queen," the boss demanded.

Jessica wavered, the color draining from her face. Maybe if she did as they said, they'd leave her alone. *Fat chance, Jess,* she thought desperately. *Once you give in to bullies, they never let up.*

Jessica shook her head, keeping her jailhouse sneakers firmly rooted to the ground. If they wanted to see her jump, they'd have to throw her up in the air.

Rerun flexed her muscular arms and took a step toward her.

Jessica stepped back. "Why are you bothering me?" she cried.

"Why are you bothering me?" Rerun mimicked evilly.

Jessica stepped backward again. But by now she was up against the wall and Rerun was still advancing, her fists clenched. Jessica tried to squirm to her left, but Rerun gave her a hard shove, causing Jessica to scrape her tender skin against the rough cement wall.

"Ow!" Jessica cried out in pain, and flung herself against the woman. But Rerun was like a block of stone. She grabbed Jessica by the arms and sent her reeling across the tiny cell, where she collapsed onto her cot. Before she could get to her feet, Rerun and the boss were above her, sadistic smiles curled on their lips.

The boss brought her face down only inches from Jessica's. "We don't like pretty little girls," she whispered. "So it's time for your makeover."

Jessica squeezed her eyes shut and put her

arms up to block the blows. *Here it comes,* she thought, terrified, bracing herself. *Now they're going to finish me off.*

Oh no! Celine thought, her hand shaking as she ripped open the letter from the credit card company. It had been lying there on the mat outside her front door waiting for her. The red Final Notice stamp on the envelope clearly warned her of what was in store.

"What?" she gasped, quickly scanning the letter. "They're only giving me three more days! How can I possibly come up with the money that soon?"

She sank down onto her tattered living-room couch. "Why can't they repossess this junk?" she moaned. She hung her head, letting her honey blond curls spill across her face. "I'm ruined," she sobbed. "In three days I'll be kicked out of the Thetas."

She could easily imagine the glee on Isabella, Alex, and Jessica's faces. *Not Jessica,* she reminded herself. The one bright spot in all of this. "I might be socially ruined, but her whole life is ruined!"

At least she'll have a life. Celine's mind raced to the honed edge of Scarface's switchblade. "If I don't get some money," she wailed, "I won't even have that!"

Celine reached anxiously for the phone and her last hope. Granny Boudreaux had to come through for her now. Her only granddaughter's life was at stake.

The phone rang for ages before a cultured voice picked it up. "Boudreaux residence," the man said, his vowels perfectly enunciated. "Whom, may I ask, is calling?" Granny Boudreaux always hired highly educated Yankees as her servants. She liked to take her revenge where she could.

"Walters, it's me, Celine. Is Granny there?"

"Hello, Miss Celine, I'll see if Madame Boudreaux is receiving calls this evening."

Celine sighed and rolled her dark blue eyes. Granny treated all her calls practically like social visits. If she had her way, she'd instruct the butler to whip up a batch of fresh mint juleps and have her maid dress her in finery before accepting a call.

After what seemed like hours the phone was picked up again.

"Granny?" Celine said. "I need—"

"I'm sorry, Miss Celine," Walters interrupted. "Madame Boudreaux did not wish to be disturbed."

"Disturbed?" Celine exploded. "I'm her granddaughter! I must talk to her."

"I'm sorry, miss—"

"Walters," Celine insisted, feeling a trickle of

fear at the base of her spine. "I've got to talk to her. I'm in trouble. Tell her that."

"I'm sorry, miss," Walters repeated, his voice kind but implacable. "It saddens me to hear you are distressed. But Madame Boudreaux said under no circumstances."

"Walters," Celine gasped, her knuckles turning white as she gripped the phone. "You get Granny right now. This is life and death!"

Walters cleared his throat. "Madame said, 'Under no circumstances, especially life and death,'" he intoned courteously. "Perhaps you could try again after Madame Boudreaux has had her nap?"

"Walters," Celine cried, her heart beating wildly, her breath coming out in short, panicked gasps, "that might be too late."

"In that case, Miss Celine," Walters replied graciously. "Let me say now, it has been a pleasure knowing you."

"Back off." A voice, tough and sharp as a gunshot, rang through Jessica's cell. "Touch her and you'll have to deal with me!"

Jessica snapped open her eyes and peered around. Above her Rerun had dropped her fists, and her ruddy complexion had turned pale. But Jessica couldn't see the person who had stood up for her. Then suddenly both

Rerun and the boss woman stumbled out of her cell and took off.

Jessica now had a clear view of her savior. The woman looked middle-aged, with graying hair and a deep scowl. Jessica had never seen her face before, but she recognized her voice and the red garnet ring shining on her little finger.

"Marian," Jessica cried, stumbling away from the cot and throwing herself into the older woman's arms. She'd never been so relieved to see anyone before.

Marian's face broke into a grin, her pale blue eyes sparkling. "I hoped I'd find you, kid. It looks like I got here just in time. Are you OK?"

Jessica shook her head, her body still shaking. "I guess so. But why were they bothering me?"

Marian shrugged. "You're the new girl on the block. They tried it with me when I arrived this morning. But I showed them I'd give as good as they gave. I didn't get away from one abusive situation to end up in another."

Jessica nodded and scuffed the floor with her sneaker. "I wish I could say the same. I'm not much of a fighter."

Marian threw her arm around Jessica's shoulders. "Don't worry, kid. Now that they know you have a friend, they won't be bothering you again."

"Thanks, Marian." Jessica smiled.

"And anyway," Marian added. "Your indictment hearing is tomorrow. After that you'll be out of here."

Jessica slumped her shoulders. If only it were that easy. "I don't know, Marian," she mumbled. "It doesn't look good. No one's been able to find any hard evidence on my behalf."

Marian rubbed her chin. "That's a tough one, kid. But come on, let's go eat. You can tell me all about it over dinner."

Jessica followed Marian through the crowded jailhouse cafeteria, holding out her tray as hard-bitten workers indiscriminately slopped food on her plate, assembly-line style. "What is this?" she asked, trying not to gag.

Marian rolled her eyes. "Don't ask. Just eat. It's easier if you breathe through your mouth."

Jessica took a seat next to Marian at the long, Formica-topped dining table and pushed away her plate. "Blech." Chez Louis, this was not.

A heavy woman sitting diagonally across from them shot out her hand. "Finished?"

Jessica raised one eyebrow and nodded.

The woman grabbed the plate, dumped the contents onto her own, and began furiously eating.

Jessica winced and turned away. Was that going to be her in ten years?

She turned back to Marian. "Nick's giving me the benefit of the doubt." She sighed. "That's it. He still needs proof."

Marian swallowed the last of her brown mush and then put down her fork. "That's better than nothing."

Jessica hung her head, and her long blond hair swung into her face. She didn't have the energy to brush it away. "I love Nick," she said in a trembling voice. "I don't think I'm ever going to see him again." Tears began to fill her eyes.

"Oh, kid," Marian murmured. "Don't let it get you down. You've got to stay tough."

Jessica shook her head. "I can't help it. Nick means everything to me. But now it's all over. I'm going to spend the rest of my life in jail." The tears were now streaming down her face.

Marian pushed away her tray and took Jessica's hand. "Stop it," she said harshly. "You'll never survive prison if you act like this."

"I don't care," Jessica sobbed. "My life is ruined. I just want to die!"

"Hey, Liz, wait up!" Elizabeth stopped on the path leading to Dickenson Hall, turning toward the familiar-sounding voice.

Alex and Noah jogged toward her.

Alex reached her first, slightly out of breath. "We were just looking for you."

Elizabeth ran a hand over her forehead. "I was visiting Jess," she said glumly.

Alex bowed her head, her deep green eyes full of compassion. "How is she?"

Elizabeth shrugged and smoothed out a wrinkle in her pleated skirt. "Not too good. The county jail is an awful place." Elizabeth could feel fresh tears waiting behind her eyes. "There's got to be a way to get her out of there."

"We might be able to help," Noah said, panting as he caught up to them. "We have information. We were hoping you could tell us how to find Nick Fox."

"Nick?" Elizabeth asked. "I need to talk to him too. Jessica remembered that the guy who gave her the package was tall and skinny and wearing an SVU Engineering sweatshirt."

"Great," Alex enthused. "That really narrows the search." She quickly filled Elizabeth in on the mystery hot-line caller.

"Let me change," Elizabeth said excitedly, "and we can all go down to the police station."

Noah shook his head, a lock of his shaggy blond hair spilling into his face. "Nick's not there. We already tried. The police chief said he's gone. Though whether that means left town or left the force, he wouldn't say."

"What?" Elizabeth cried, twisting the strap of her pocketbook. How could that be? She'd seen

Nick a few hours ago. He'd seemed determined to help Jessica. "That doesn't make any sense."

But before Noah had a chance to answer, Elizabeth gasped. Coming down the path toward them was Tom with an armful of books and a girl at his side. The girl's face was turned toward him, so her dark brown hair hid her features.

Elizabeth involuntarily took a step back. *Tom with another woman?* She felt the air squeeze out of her lungs. If there had been a tree or a building, she would have jumped behind it. But she, Alex, and Noah were standing in the middle of the quad with only lush expanses of grass about them.

Tom still hadn't seen her as the distance between them was rapidly closing. He was looking only at the girl, laughing and gesturing with his free hand. *Did I mean so little to him that he's replaced me already?* she thought wretchedly, a moan escaping from her lips. She swallowed hard and braced herself for the meeting. Suddenly Tom looked up and their eyes met. The laugh immediately died in his throat and his smiling eyes hardened.

"Tom," Elizabeth murmured, her heart slamming against her chest.

"Hi, Liz," the girl said sweetly.

Elizabeth started at the sound of her voice.

It's Nancy, she realized, turning to her. *Tom's lab partner. Not a new girlfriend!*

A small smile crossed her lips. "Tom," she said again, relief pouring into her. But Tom didn't even nod. Instead he plowed past her, head bent as if he'd never known her at all.

"Come on, Nancy," he barked. "Or we'll be late for class."

Nancy looked at Elizabeth awkwardly, obviously unsure of what was happening. Finally she turned and hurried after Tom.

Elizabeth felt her knees give out. She would have staggered to the ground if Noah hadn't caught her under the arm and led her to a bench.

"Liz, I'm so sorry," Alex murmured, shock registering on her face. She slipped down onto the bench and wrapped her arm around Elizabeth's trembling shoulders. "I thought this trouble with Jess might bring you two back together."

Elizabeth shook her head in a daze, her whole body shaking. Noah squeezed her arm. "Don't give up hope, Liz. You and Tom will find a way to work things out."

"No," Elizabeth sobbed, rising from the bench and pushing past them to run to her dorm room. "Nothing short of a miracle will get us back together."

128

* * *

"Hello?" Alex called as she entered Theta house. "Anyone here?" After an hour's fruitless search for Nick, she and Noah had given up for the evening. There was a big Zeta party that night, and Alex had promised some of the Zetas she knew that she'd round up her fellow Theta sisters to attend. She poked her head in the parlor. "Celine Boudreaux's den of iniquity," she scoffed to herself. No one, not even Celine and her self-satisfied smirk, was there. Though the telltale smell of Celine's gardenia perfume hung in the room like a San Francisco fog.

Alex checked the kitchen. There were no cups on the granite table, and the cappuccino maker was put away. The sink sparkled and even the Formica-top counter had been wiped clean. There wasn't so much as a crumb to prove anyone lived there.

She redoubled her efforts and searched the TV and game lounge, the small sunroom off the parlor, and the basement laundry. Nothing. Not a soul. Finally she ended up in the den. It was Alex's favorite place in Theta house. This was the room where the girls gathered to study together. Alex stifled a giggle. *More like gab together,* she thought, *if last semester's grades were anything to go by.* No one was studying there now. The wooden chairs stood neatly under the desks. Not even a pad of paper was out of place.

Alex tossed her long auburn hair over her shoulder and sighed. "I've never seen Theta house this deserted," she murmured to herself. She thought quickly of all the functions going on around campus that evening. There was the big Cary Grant retrospective playing at the movie house. The Pi Beta Phi sorority house was having a party. There was a new jazz combo playing at the café in town. And the Zetas were throwing their monthly bash.

"Of course no one's here," Alex scolded herself. "Everyone is already there!"

Suddenly she heard a big *clunk* from upstairs. *Well, not everybody,* she thought. Alex headed for the carpeted staircase, taking the steps two at a time. She started down the right side of the hallway, where the girls' bedrooms were, only to realize the noises were coming from the left. *But that's the old storage room,* she thought. *Why would anyone be in there?*

Alex didn't stop to consider as she headed for the room. The noise intensified as if someone were walking around blindly, banging into the old suitcases and cast-off furniture. She stopped in front of the door. The hairs on the back of her neck were standing up and her heart was racing. There was no light coming from under it. Someone was in there in the dark.

Alex reached out a shaky hand. "It's nothing," she whispered to herself. "Just push open the door. The light must have burned out and one of the girls is trapped in there." *Then why don't I call out to them?* she thought, her throat suddenly dry.

There was another loud bang, and Alex jumped back. *Maybe I'll go get help,* she thought. But no one was around. It could take ages before she found someone and got them to come back.

She took a deep breath to steady her nerves and pushed open the door. The room was pitch black. She blinked a few times, trying to get her eyes accustomed to the lack of light. Then from the back of the room, where the girls stored their steamer trunks, bicycles, and skiing gear, she spied a small pinprick of light. It was a flashlight. But what Theta would use a flashlight when all she had to do was change the bulb? *None,* Alex realized with a start. *The person I'm alone with in this room must be a burglar!*

She let out a bloodcurdling scream and backed toward the door. "*Burglar!*" she hollered. But the words were all but strangled in her throat as a strong, forceful hand roughly clamped itself across her mouth.

Chapter
Eight

Nick's long, lean body tensed and he shot to his feet as a girl's terrified scream pierced the blackness around him. In two quick strides he was across the dark, cluttered room. He roughly grabbed the girl, clamping a hand over her mouth to cut off a fresh shriek.

"I'm not a burglar," Nick said between clenched teeth. "My name is Nick Fox. I'm a police officer." He hoped that would silence her or he was in big trouble. Breaking and entering was a serious offense. Now that he'd been suspended from the force, they'd probably throw the book at him! He had to think fast.

"Are you alone?"

The girl nodded frantically.

Nick hesitated. She could be lying. He strained his eyes for any other silhouettes that might be lurking in the dark, his flashlight lying impotently at his feet. *You can't stay here like this all night, Nick,* he thought. No one else seemed to be there now, but eventually they would be.

"Please don't scream again," he appealed to the girl. "I'm here to help Jessica Wakefield." Nick loosened the pressure over the girl's mouth by a fraction, ready to grab her again if she so much as took a deep breath.

Instead, to his surprise, she took his hand and led him out of the cramped storage room.

"Nick. Thank goodness I found you," the girl said, relief flooding her voice. She looked up at him, smiling shakily.

"Alex," Nick said, realizing who it was now that they were in the light. "What is it?"

Alex shuddered, looking over at the darkened storage room. "Let's go downstairs first," she said with a small laugh.

Nick gritted his teeth. He didn't have time for small talk. It was almost eight P.M. Each moment was ticking closer to Jessica's indictment hearing in the morning, and he still didn't have a shred of evidence to help her. "If this can wait—"

"No," Alex cut in. "It's very important, Nick."

She led him into a comfortable room full of old leather chairs with a large wooden partner desk in the middle. "Look, Alex," he said curtly.

"If this is about alcohol, I think you should call the hot line—"

"It's about Jessica," Alex said quickly, dropping down on the couch and curling her legs up under her. She had his attention now. Nick grabbed a chair, straddling it across from her.

"I got a disturbing call at the hot line." She hesitated, running a hand through her wavy auburn hair. "I know it's supposed to be confidential, but with Jessica in jail, I think it's more important that I tell you what happened."

Nick leaned toward her. "I want to hear anything you know about Jessica's case. But not if it's going to jeopardize the confidentiality of the hot line."

Alex bit her lip. "There are no names. I've thought a lot about this. The caller I spoke to was being coerced. I think it was more a cry for help than anything else."

Nick squeezed the back of the chair. "OK. What do you know?" Finally he was getting somewhere.

Alex took a breath and then started. "Twice this guy has called. First to say he suspected he was about to become involved in a drug exchange and then to say there had been one."

Nick tried to hide his excitement, but his hand was shaking as he pulled a notebook from his leather jacket and flipped it open. "When did he call?" he asked, uncapping his pen.

"Tuesday and then again earlier today."

Nick nodded, his mind racing. The day of the drug exchange and the day after it. If this guy wasn't involved, how could he have known exactly when the drug deal had happened? "What else did he say?"

Alex sat up, hugging her knees to her chest. "He went on and on about how he didn't want any part of it. That his domineering girlfriend was making him do it."

Nick's heart sank. *Girlfriend?* he thought. *Could that mean Jessica?*

As if reading his mind, Alex shook her head. "This girl threatened him after Jessica was already in jail."

"Do you know who he was talking about?"

Alex shifted in her seat. "Maybe. I think it might be Celine Boudreaux."

Nick remembered Celine. Honey blond curls and makeup so thick her face looked like porcelain. And, he recalled with an involuntary sneeze, the stench of overripe flowers. "Why her?"

Alex frowned. "It's just a hunch. But the guy on the phone said when he did the exchange, the woman gave him a hatbox with a big, floppy white hat in it."

Nick's pulse quickened. Jessica had mentioned something about a hatbox. *Could it be the same one?* They were getting close. He could feel it.

"Today at our Theta party," Alex continued, "Celine was wearing that exact type of hat. And Lila Fowler thought she recognized the hat as the one Jessica was supposed to pick up for her earlier this week."

"Great work, Alex," Nick enthused. "This could put Jessica in the clear. But I've got to find that caller. What else did he tell you?"

Alex clasped her hands. "He said he was scared. Really scared. That the woman was going to turn him over to the mobsters she got the drugs from if he went to the police. He's running away to a small town on the coast where his family lives."

Nick tilted his chair forward. "Did he say which town?"

Alex shook her head sadly. "Not even if it was north or south from here."

Nick closed his eyes. He didn't have any hard evidence of Jessica's innocence yet, but now he knew there was someone to look for. Jessica's mystery man really *did* exist.

"But I have one more piece of information."

Nick opened his eyes to see a smile spreading across Alex's face. "I talked to Elizabeth. Jessica remembered that the guy was wearing an SVU Engineering sweatshirt."

Nick jumped to his feet. "Great, Alex! This

may be the break we've been looking for!"

Nick practically skipped out of Theta house, his heart lighter than it had been in days. *Finally I have a few leads,* he thought. *Hang on, Jess. It won't be long now!*

Elizabeth threw down her pen in frustration and punched her pillow. "What's the use?" she told her empty dorm room. "Tom hates me. Writing down my feelings isn't going to change that!"

Elizabeth pushed her journal aside and sprang from her bed. "I'm going crazy staring at these lonely four walls," she cried. "At least outside, I'll be alone with a crowd." She grabbed her jean jacket and headed for the door.

Out on the quad the velvety sky glittered with stars. With such a romantic night, Elizabeth couldn't help but think of Tom. "There was so much love between us, it's hard to believe it won't win out," she whispered.

Elizabeth's aquamarine eyes traveled up the walk to the facade of the WSVU building. *Is Tom in there now?* she wondered. When they were together, they always worked late into the evening. "Worked?" She laughed a little to herself, thinking of all the time they'd spent kissing, locked in each other's arms. *It's a wonder we ever had a story to broadcast!*

Elizabeth closed her eyes, suddenly feeling close to tears. "Will I ever be in your arms again?" she murmured.

A gentle hand touched her shoulder. "Liz, are you all right?"

Elizabeth jumped, spinning around to find Alex and Noah standing before her. "Oh, hey . . . ," she said, quickly wiping a tear from her eye. "I was just—"

"It's OK," Alex said gently. "We saw you over here and thought you might want some company."

Elizabeth grimaced. "Do I look that miserable?"

Noah laughed. "Not too bad. But we have some information that might cheer you up."

Elizabeth widened her eyes expectantly.

"I saw Nick," Alex related. "I told him about my mystery hot-line caller and gave him Jessica's description of the guy. He's sure he can do something to help Jessica now."

"Great," Elizabeth enthused. "Finally we're getting somewhere."

Alex and Noah nodded happily.

"Liz," Noah said, "we're off to a party at Zeta house. Why don't you come along with us?"

Elizabeth bit her lip. It sounded tempting, but would she really be much fun with her thoughts full of Tom? "Thanks, but I don't think so. I think I'd be better off staying at home."

"Are you sure?" Alex asked. "It might make you feel better."

"Yeah," Noah added. "A little fun could do you good."

Elizabeth looked at her two friends and shrugged. "Until my heart mends a little, I'm not going to be good company for anyone. But I'll walk you that way."

The three of them headed toward Greek Row, where the sorority and fraternity houses stood. From the Pi Beta Phi sorority Elizabeth could hear a party in full swing. Light, music, and laughter spilled out from the front door, and happy groups of students caroused outside on the pavement.

"Are you sure we can't change your mind?" Noah asked as the ivy-clad walls of Zeta house loomed before them.

Elizabeth smiled faintly and shook her head. She was about to start toward her dorm when she suddenly spotted Tom and Danny as they turned down the path toward them. She ducked behind Noah's muscular frame. *Why did I do that?* she questioned herself, her heart pounding and her palms sweaty. *Why did I hide?*

Elizabeth tossed back her blond ponytail, anger building inside her. The answer was all too obvious. Tom was laughing and slapping Danny on the back as if he didn't have a care in the world. The same carefree way he'd been with Nancy, his lab partner. She couldn't bear being snubbed by him again.

Elizabeth clenched her jaw, fuming as Tom and Danny sprang up the steps to the Pi Beta house. Tom certainly wasn't mooning around campus, thinking about the good times he'd had with her.

She turned to Alex and Noah, her outrage boiling over. "On second thought," she announced furiously, "I'd love to go to the Zeta party!" If Tom could get on with his life so easily, then so could she. Elizabeth Wakefield was a free woman and she was going to party until she dropped!

"My father's the greatest." Tom laughed, clapping Danny on the back as they strolled up the path to Pi Beta Phi house. "We spent all afternoon watching the sports channel. He's got a satellite dish that brings in games from all over the world. We even watched a soccer game from Ecuador."

"Man," Danny said, shaking his head. "My dad never does anything with me. I'd love to have a father I could hang out with."

"Yeah, it's great," Tom enthused. "And we talk. Man-to-man. I feel like I could tell him anything and he'd understand. He's really there for me."

"Wow," Danny said. "That's another thing I wish I had. I can be away for the whole semester and my dad still only grunts when I walk into the room. Like he hadn't even noticed I was gone."

Tom smiled. "Come with us, then. My dad thinks the more the merrier. He's getting tickets for the Rams game tomorrow. I'll tell him to get you one."

Danny shook his head. "It sounds great. But I can't. Jessica's trial is tomorrow—I want to be there for her."

Tom scowled. *Figures,* he thought. *I finally get a chance to see the Rams play and something Wakefield related ruins it.* He felt a dark cloud settle over his good mood as the picture of Elizabeth's distressed eyes flashed across his mind.

Danny gave him a sideways glance. "We're here, Tom," he said lightly. "Are you still up for this?"

Tom looked up at the sorority house standing before them. Its foundation was practically rocking. Through the large bay window he could see couples spinning around the living-room floor. The music was loud and raucous. And everywhere people were milling about, laughing, singing, drinking, and having a great time.

Tom wanted to be a part of it, but the image in his mind of Elizabeth made him hesitate. She needed him now. Shouldn't he be with her? But then a stronger image came to mind, the one of his father's crumpled face when Tom had told him about Elizabeth's accusation. *No*, Tom thought, shaking his head. *Liz forfeited my support when she tried to destroy my relationship with my father.*

"Let's go for it," Tom pronounced, and he and Danny bounded up the steps.

"Better take it easy on that punch." A deep voice snickered at Elizabeth over the pulsating music of the Zeta house party. "It'll go right to your head."

Elizabeth turned and made a face at two Zeta fraternity brothers who were gawking at her and laughing. When would clods like that stop making fun of people who didn't drink alcohol? There was nothing wrong with drinking punch at a party. *If I was on the beer line, they wouldn't have said word one to me,* she thought.

Elizabeth looked around. The Zeta party was in full swing, alive with laughter, blasting music, and animated talk. "Forget those losers, Liz," she told herself. "Just enjoy yourself." She finished off her second large punch and helped herself to another one. She was hot and thirsty from the crowded, sweltering room and all she'd done so far was squeeze through the dancing mob to the buffet table.

If Tom and I were still together, Elizabeth's mind wandered, *we'd be one of those couples dancing.* She imagined them spinning together in the middle of the room, her golden hair fanning out around her face. Afterward they would sneak off to a secluded corner where they could talk and snuggle. Elizabeth felt a sharp stab in her heart. Was Tom in a secluded corner at the Pi Beta party with some other girl right now?

She gulped the rest of her punch. *This party isn't helping me at all,* she thought miserably. She took a step toward the nearby garbage pail and suddenly felt very strange.

Whoa! she thought. Her cowboy boots felt like they were filled with lead. She was dizzy, her head spinning crazily. She stumbled, falling into the bigger of the two Zetas. His beer sloshed down the front of his football jersey.

"Whoops," he said with a laugh. He hoisted her off him, steadying her on her feet. "Told you to watch that punch. It packs a wallop."

Elizabeth brushed him away. "Stop saying that," she managed, her voice sounding slurred and far away. She turned and started to stumble across the packed dance floor. *What's wrong with me?* she thought. *Maybe it's the crowd. It's awfully cramped in here. I need some fresh air.*

A hard, sweaty body smacked against her, sending her sprawling into a group of frenzied dancers. One of them pushed her back, and she staggered against two other people. Finally she made her way to the side of the room, where she clung to the back of an easy chair.

"What's happening to me?" she gasped. The whole room seemed to be spinning. The music pounded in her ears. Suddenly the lights went down and a strobe started up, sending out quick, blinding pulses that made her even more dizzy and nauseous. *I've been poisoned!* flashed through her mind.

"Hey, watch it," a shrill voice screamed. Elizabeth felt her grip on the chair give way and she was nearly drawn back onto the dance floor. The gyrating bodies were like a big eggbeater, trying to pull her into the middle of the room. Elizabeth cried out. She flung herself against the wall and inched along until she reached an alcove.

"A nice secluded corner," she murmured weakly. But no Tom to share it with. "Where are you, Tom?" she cried.

Suddenly the Zeta whose beer she'd spilled pushed into the alcove with her. She looked up at him, feeling her vision blur. He was at least three times her size—huge, hulking, and muscular.

Elizabeth shrank back as his hot breath, reeking of alcohol, wafted toward her face.

"I'm Pete," he bellowed into her ear.

Elizabeth winced and pulled away, her stomach doing a quick flip. But that backed her deeper into the corner.

"I told you not to drink so much punch," he slurred. "Me and Joey just finished spiking it."

That explained why she felt so strange! *I'm drunk!* Elizabeth thought. She closed her eyes and a giggle escaped from her throat. *I'm just drunk!* "Why didn't you tell me?" she mumbled, her tongue as thick as cotton wool.

Pete laughed and wrapped a heavy arm around her shoulders. "I did," he slobbered, pulling her close to him. "That's why I'm with you now. To make sure you're OK."

Elizabeth smiled, her head spinning. It felt good to be cared for. "That's nice," she slurred. "You like me. Tom doesn't. He hates me." She started to slide down the wall.

Pete laughed and lodged his arms under hers, pulling her up like a rag doll. "Who cares about Tom? You've got Pete now." He pulled one of his arms away to point a wavering finger at his chest. "Pete. That's me."

Elizabeth started to fall again. "This wall is slippery," she hiccuped.

Pete grinned and yanked her toward him,

crushing her against his chest. Elizabeth looked up at him. Two faces looked back at her with big, sloppy grins. *Nice grins,* she thought. *He likes me. Not like Tom.* She rested her head against Pete's big chest. She felt awfully sleepy.

Pete pulled her arms around his neck and she dropped her head down onto his shoulder.

"Not like that," he said with a laugh. He lifted her chin and started planting wet, mushy kisses in the vicinity of her mouth.

Blech, Elizabeth thought as he soaked her face. *This guy is gross.* But her head felt so heavy, she could barely lift it. She'd never be able to make it to the door. She doubted she could even get her feet to try.

Pete let go of her head, and it slumped against his chest again. It didn't feel right there. None of this felt right. But she was tired. And at least Pete's arms were holding her up. He leaned in for another kiss. *What difference does it make what it feels like?* she thought groggily. *My life's a complete mess anyway.*

Chapter Nine

"There's got to be something worth stealing here," Celine muttered anxiously as she rummaged through the last bedroom in Theta house. It was late, and the girls might return any moment. She had to be quick. She wrenched a drawer out of Gloria Abel's nightstand and overturned it. A few pieces of jewelry rolled across the floor. Celine dove for them, holding a pair of earrings under her flashlight. "Paste," she said disgustedly, crinkling her nose. She tossed them aside.

This burglary was a huge disappointment. Apparently none of her Theta sisters had anything of value. She'd found two promising-looking picture frames in Pam Stanger's room, but they'd turned out to be gold plated. And Kimberly Schyler's paintings had been nothing but shoddy reproductions. Celine rolled her eyes.

"I thought these girls were supposed to be well off," she announced contemptuously. "I think I've joined a sorority full of poseurs!"

Wait a minute! she remembered. There was a safe downstairs in the main room. "Of course, these girls would keep their valuables locked up."

Celine swiftly flew down the stairs. If the safe was anything like Granny Boudreaux's old tumbler model, she should be able to open it. But she had to hurry. Being found in the dark, dressed in black with a flashlight in her hand, would not be an easy thing to explain. And the way she felt now, with her heart pounding and her body on the verge of panic, explaining was the last thing she wanted to do.

She got to the safe and dropped to her knees. It was an enormous metal box like Granny's, but that was where the similarity ended. The face of this safe had three electronically coded locks and a red sensor light. Which meant one wrong number and the police would be summoned.

Celine sighed and sat back on her heels. She might have turned burglar, but she didn't have the skills of a top-notch safecracker.

She turned off her flashlight and felt her way

in the dark to the front door. She'd run out of time. *And luck,* she thought despondently.

"Ow," she screamed, banging into something hard in the foyer. She snapped on her flashlight. It was the writing desk where Magda Helperin, the president of the Thetas, sat when she was working on sorority business. Celine opened the top drawer. Maybe she'd find a little money set aside for the deliverymen. It wouldn't be enough to pay off any of her debts, but at least she could get her next meal. She shone her flashlight on the contents and pushed some papers aside. Rent slips, a cleaning schedule, a ledger on the house dues, and an envelope addressed to Lila Fowler.

"Now what is this?" she murmured, picking it up between two fingers. Something stiff inside it slid to the bottom. Celine felt the outline of the object through the envelope. It felt like a card. "Like maybe," she whispered, her pulse beginning to race as she ripped open the envelope, "a bank card!"

Bingo! The precious object fell to the tiled floor. Celine scooped it up and read the note attached. "Lila—I found this on the quad—Isabella."

Perfect! Celine licked her lips. Who knew how long ago the card had been lost? If she took that down to the bank first thing tomorrow morning, she could get her money and return the card before anyone knew she'd been near it. Everyone would think it had been used before Isabella found it.

"I'm saved!" Celine gushed. "And with a credit line like Lila's, I'll be able to pay off Scarface and his gang, my credit card debts, and still have a little money on the side! A nice shopping spree along Rodeo Drive is just the thing to help me forget this nasty little near-death experience."

"Hi there!" A cute girl with short black hair and laughing green eyes gave Tom a hundred-watt smile.

Tom felt his eyes widen. "Hi there to you too," he shouted over the throbbing music in the Pi Beta house. This party was definitely looking up.

"Want to dance?" the girl yelled, pulling his arm.

"Why not?" Tom responded. Danny had abandoned him at least half an hour ago to dance with his girlfriend, Isabella.

The girl led him to the dance floor and clamped her slender arms around his neck like a vise. *Whoa!* Tom thought. This girl was practically climbing into his lap. Not an easy feat since he was standing.

"I'm Patty," she chattered, "and you're fantastic. You're the cutest thing I've ever seen. You're—"

"Thirsty," Tom cut in, removing her arms from around his neck. "I need a drink." *And a little breathing room.*

Patty released him reluctantly, shoving her bottom lip out in a pout. "Come on, then," she offered, motioning him toward her with her index finger. "I'll show you where the beer is."

Tom felt doubtful but followed her anyway. Maybe he'd bump into Danny on the way and then he could give Patty the slip. The girl pulled him through the crowded hallway and in and out of several rooms, each one more crammed than the last.

"I hope you know where you're going," Tom shouted to her over the throbbing music. After being led through that confusing maze, he was afraid he'd never find his way out.

Patty gave him an impish grin and kept bouncing along on her ballet slippers. Finally they burst into the kitchen, where a large keg of beer was propped in a corner. A bunch of Sigmas were looming over it.

Tom walked up and poured himself a plastic cup of beer. He turned to Patty. "Do you want one?"

She wrinkled her nose. "I'm high on life," she

151

said with a giggle, and spun around on her slippers. Her long, sheer skirt twirled around her.

The frat boys laughed and whistled, and Tom felt the blood rising to his face. He hoped no one thought they were together. This girl was an absolute ditz.

Tom lifted his hand to take a gulp of his beer. Like lightning, Patty ducked under his arm and came up pressing flat against his body. Tom started, spitting his beer on the floor. The Sigmas laughed even louder.

Patty gave him a wide smile and nuzzled against his chest. "You're cute."

Tom held up both his arms and stepped back. *Just my luck,* he thought, *she's certifiable.*

"Patty, leave the nice man alone." The woman's voice was cosmopolitan, her accent vaguely European. "He seems overwhelmed."

Tom looked over at the owner of the voice, a sinewy brunette who was perched on the kitchen counter. She took a long drag of her cigarette and expelled smoke through her nose. "Unless you like that sort of attention?" She raised a shapely eyebrow over her dark brown eyes.

Tom gulped. The young woman staring back at him was miles more sophisticated than the girls he'd seen so far at this party. She was dressed in a smart royal blue linen suit. Her shapely legs were crossed, one high heel dangling from her toe. Her glittering eyes mocked him.

"No, I—" Tom started.

The woman turned to Patty. "Run along, pet. You're frightening our guest."

Patty giggled and skipped out of the room, the contingency of frat boys following her. Tom and the mystery woman were now alone in the kitchen.

She smiled and held out her hand. "I'm Claudia."

"Tom," he said, shaking her hand. *This is more like it,* he thought. At least he had someone rational to talk to now.

Claudia toyed with a strand of her silky dark hair. "Are you alone, Tom?" she asked.

Tom took a sip of his beer. "I came with a friend. But I lost him when Patty took me captive."

Claudia laughed. "Hmmm. I like that." She smiled, fresh smoke curling from between her lips. "Does that mean there's no little woman back in her dorm room waiting for your call?"

Tom frowned. *What business is it of yours?* he thought.

"Well, Tom?" she prompted.

An image of Elizabeth's expectant face, her hand hovering above the phone, flashed through his mind. *Is she waiting for me?* he wondered. Tom shook his head. No. Their breakup had been final.

Claudia raised her eyebrow again and pulled a piece of tobacco from her lip. "That didn't seem very definitive, Tom. Want to try it again?"

Tom made a face. Where was this girl coming from? At first he'd liked her straightforward approach, but now it seemed intrusive. "Try what again?" he asked.

"Convincing me you're really footloose and fancy free."

"Why would I want to do that?" he asked. As attractive and mysterious as Claudia was, her pushy attitude was beginning to get on his nerves.

Claudia threw back her head and laughed. "Lighten up, Tom. This is the getting-to-know-you stage. I tease you a little. You tease me. We play, what do you Americans call them—head games?"

Tom winced. Game playing was something he and Elizabeth had never gone through. Sure, there had been a few crossed signals as they got to know each other. But neither one of them had intentionally toyed with the other. They'd respected each other, and their respect had easily turned to love.

Tom gritted his teeth. He'd hoped socializing would help him forget, make him stop obsessing over Elizabeth. But this party was having the opposite effect. *I miss her,* he thought. It wasn't fair. Why should he have to go through the whole dating game again? *Because Elizabeth betrayed you!* his mind shot back.

Tom shrugged and looked up at the woman sitting above him. "Sorry, Claudia. I just went through the it's-all-over stage with somebody else. I'm not really ready for the getting-to-know-you stage yet."

She tossed her cigarette in the sink and stood up. "That's OK, Tommy. I like a man on the rebound."

Tom took a step back. "Well, I think I need a few more bounces before I'm ready to be picked up." He turned and headed toward the door of the kitchen. It was obviously going to be a while before he'd be ready to date again. In fact, until Elizabeth Wakefield was completely out of his system, socializing might be the worst thing for him.

"Come back when you're ready, Tommy," he heard Claudia call from over his shoulder. "I play a mean game of one-on-one."

"This is all wrong," Elizabeth slurred, her words lost in the dance music that blasted through

Zeta house. Her face was squashed against Pete's sweaty football jersey, and she could barely breathe. Her head was throbbing from the effort to stay conscious, and her legs were like jelly. All she really wanted to do was close her eyes and drop off. *But not here,* she thought, and began to cry. *I've got to get outside.*

Pete swooped down on her with a laugh, his wet lips smacking against her sore cheek. He started to pull at her chin with his fingers, guiding her lips toward his. She turned her head and weakly tried to push him away.

"Stop it!" she said with a groan. She fought to clear her head, but each time her eyes tried to focus, the room began to spin. At any moment she was afraid she'd be sick.

"Don't you like Pete anymore?" he slobbered.

Save me, Elizabeth thought helplessly. *Please, someone get me out of here.* It was an effort just to keep her head up. She started to slip and tightened her grip on Pete's arms to keep from falling.

"That's more like it," he gurgled in her hair, catching the side of her forehead with a wet, soggy kiss.

Elizabeth felt his big, meaty hand travel down her back and start to tug at her bra. *Oh no!* Warning bells rang in her head. *I've got to make him stop.* She started to struggle and pull back, but his giant arms and her drunken condition made it impossible to move.

Pete gripped her tighter, crushing her wobbly body against him. His hands were freely groping her. "Oh, baby, you feel so good," he drooled. "I knew you wanted me."

The small sober part of her mind screamed out, *Run! This is wrong! Get away from this loser!* But the signal didn't reach her limbs as she remained captured in his grasp, her body mauled by his roving hands.

Suddenly Pete's grip lessened, and Elizabeth felt herself begin to fall. She had nearly collapsed onto the floor when another pair of hands pulled her up. This pair was steady and gentle.

"It's OK, Liz. I'll get you out of here," a kind voice murmured, stroking the sweaty hair from her face. "Beat it," she heard in a much harsher tone. Then she felt Pete's oppressive bulk retreat.

"Hold on, now," the voice said. Suddenly she felt her feet leave the ground. Was she floating? *No,* she thought, *someone is carrying me.*

Elizabeth forced her tired eyes to open a crack.

"Todd," she cried, relief flooding through her body. Todd was carrying her! He whisked her effortlessly from the tiny alcove and across the crowded dance floor. She dropped her head on his shoulder, no longer able to keep her eyes open.

"Don't let go," Todd instructed.

"I won't," she murmured dreamily, a smile curling on her lips.

Soon the sounds and smells of the loud, stuffy room had been replaced by cool, clean night air. Elizabeth snuggled against him. *He smells so good,* she thought, inhaling the refreshing combination of his clean skin and the slightly tangy scent of his cologne. *This feels right.* Her head fit perfectly in the nook of his shoulder.

"Thank you," she managed, her arms wrapped tightly around his neck. "Thank you for saving me." She shifted her head slightly until her lips reached the soft skin of Todd's cheek. She began to kiss him, searching for his mouth. But no matter how hard her lips searched in the darkness, she couldn't seem to find his.

"Had a bit to drink, Liz?" he teased, laughing sweetly.

Oh, Todd, she thought once more, opening her eyes to look up at him. *Why did I ever let you go?* She curled against his strong chest. "I could stay in your arms all night," she whispered. And then she felt her body fully relax and her eyes slowly close.

*　　*　　*

"I've never felt so wretched and lonely in my life," Jessica whimpered as she turned over on the creaking cot in her cell. She'd been tossing and turning for hours, unable to push the image of Nick's face from her mind. *I've never loved anyone the way I love you, Nick,* she thought desperately. "Please help me," she whispered. "Please get me out of here, Nick."

A loud snore broke through the bleakness of her thoughts and she sighed in frustration, rolling onto her other side. She yanked the threadbare blanket up to cover her ears. But that immediately sent goose bumps shivering across her skin as the chilly air hit her bare feet.

Jessica sat up dejectedly. "This is utterly hopeless," she complained. She kicked the blanket back down to cover her toes. But still she shivered.

Finally she drew her legs up underneath herself and wrapped the blanket around her body like a cocoon. *It's going to be a long, hard night,* she thought. "And this is how it's going to be for the next twelve to fifteen years if Nick doesn't finally believe me," she added out loud.

Jessica's bottom lip trembled and tears began to flow freely from her eyes. She brushed them away with the striped sleeve of her pajama top and shook her head. *With all the tears I've cried in the last two days, I can't believe I have any left.*

Jessica stood up and stretched. *Maybe if I move around a bit, get a little exercise,* she thought, *I'll be tired enough to fall asleep.* She began to run in place, her bare feet slapping on the cold concrete floor.

"Hey," a sleepy voice called out angrily. "What do you think you're doing in there?"

Jessica kept running. "I'm trying," she said between breaths, "to get tired."

"Shut up and go to sleep," another weary voice barked.

"Who's making all that noise?" a third one called out.

"It's the new girl. She's the troublemaker."

Jessica stopped and squinted into the darkened hallway outside her cell. "I'm not a troublemaker. I can't sleep."

"Guilty conscience." One of the voices snickered.

Jessica tossed back her blond hair, her eyes blazing. "I'm not guilty of anything," she proclaimed. "I shouldn't even be in here!"

"Oh, sure." Another woman laughed cruelly. "Then why did you break down crying in the cafeteria? Guilty, I say."

Jessica felt her face heating up. "That wasn't guilt," she shouted. "That was—I just felt so bad."

Two more voices erupted in laughter.

"Oh, poor baby," the same cruel voice sneered. "Feeling sorry for herself. Too weak and *guilty* to do anything but cry. Would rather give up than fight."

Jessica's mouth dropped open. *How dare they talk to me like that!* she fumed. She felt anger surging through her, wiping away any feelings of self-pity. She shot over to the bars of her cell. She'd show them. Jessica Wakefield had never given up on herself in her life. She was a strong person. She believed in herself.

She gripped the bars of her cell. "I am not weak!" she shouted. "I am not guilty!" She shook the bars, making them rattle. "I am innocent! Jessica Wakefield is innocent!"

Chapter Ten

"I'm Detective Fox," Nick announced loudly as he entered the busy SVU engineering computer lab. "Everybody listen up." He slipped out his notebook from his leather jacket and surveyed the crowded room, crammed full of long white laminated desks and PCs.

A handful of faces looked back at him. Even at the early hour of seven-thirty A.M. there were dozens of students already at work amidst the low hum of electronic equipment.

"I'm looking for an engineering student who may have disappeared in the last day or two," Nick went on. "He may have appeared agitated or upset."

A wiry guy sitting hunched in his chair in front of a PC smiled. "You mean, like, because he's paranoid you're out to get him?"

Nick narrowed his eyes. The joker was in the middle of a group of scrawny-looking guys in heavy metal T-shirts and wild hair huddled at the back of the room. They were laughing and drinking coffee from Styrofoam cups.

Nick stepped over the sheaths of tightly wrapped cable tacked to the floor to reach them as a heavyset guy in the group started to wheeze.

Nick rushed over with alarm. "Is he choking?" he asked. But then he realized the guy was laughing.

"The dude's probably surfing the Net," the heavy guy gasped.

Nick frowned. *Surfing?* he thought. Alex had told him the hot-line caller was going to his family's house along the coast. Maybe this guy was into water sports. "Where's the net? Is that a beach?"

The students exploded in laughter. "More like a state—" the wiry one spluttered.

Nick shook his head in bewilderment. *What's so funny?* he thought. He didn't have time for this nonsense. Jessica's indictment hearing was in less than two hours.

"A state of mind," the heavy one finished. He shook his plump head. "Get with the program. Your server is experiencing a serious fault."

Nick clenched his teeth. He could feel his face heating up and his anger beginning to rise. *I don't have time for riddles!* his mind screamed. But he knew he'd have to be patient. The possible involvement of an SVU engineering student was the best lead he had. He couldn't afford to blow it by losing his temper.

A student with a wispy beard started to snicker. "This guy's hard drive needs a total defrag."

"I say he needs a reboot," the wiry guy cackled.

Nick tensed. A reboot? That sounded threatening. He jumped back from the group and then swung around to face them. No one was going to give him a boot. He crouched down in a fighter's stance. He hadn't expected violence from a bunch of brainy engineering students, but he'd never heard of one dealing cocaine before either. If they wanted to get tough, he'd go for the wiry guy first.

"Detective Fox." The voice came from a PC station a few yards away. "Forget about those losers. I think I might be able to help."

Nick cautiously backed away from the group. They looked weak and out of shape, but he knew from experience that he couldn't be sure.

The student who had called him over wore wire-rimmed glasses and had a shock of carrot red hair. He held out his hand. "Larry Russell."

Nick shook it in return. "You have information?"

Larry nodded and moved his satchel and a stack of file folders from the chair next to him. "I think I know who you're talking about."

Nick sat down. "That's good. One more minute with those guys and I was about to rip out their cables and take them all downtown."

Larry laughed. "Don't mind them. They've gone virtual."

Nick rolled his eyes. "English, please."

Larry leaned back in his chair and smiled. "OK, let me put it this way. Their idea of a hot date on a Saturday night is to hook into a chat room on the I-net. Flesh and blood is a thing of the past."

Nick shook his head. "Forget it, Larry. This stuff is way over my head. Next time my division offers a computer course, though, I'm going to be the first one to sign on. Tell me what you know, slowly, so a dinosaur like me can understand."

Larry grinned. "Last week I met this guy who was working on a project similar to mine. It turned out that for the past three months we'd each been analyzing a solution to Fermat's vanished proof."

"Excuse me?" Nick interrupted. "Who's Fermat?"

165

Larry reached for one of the files and flipped it open. "Fermat was a mathematician who died a long time ago. He once wrote in the margin of a book that he'd discovered a proof for a perplexing mathematical argument. For years mathematicians, engineers, and scientists have been trying to figure out the proof."

Nick scratched his head. "How does this relate to the guy you met?"

Larry took a deep breath. "We'd joined forces to save time and we were right on the edge of a breakthrough. I'm talking about three months of painstaking work each about to bear fruit. We were supposed to meet yesterday, but he never showed up."

Nick looked at him blankly. "So? Maybe he ran this program earlier, without you."

Larry shook his head. "He couldn't. We each had our own disks. Neither of us could run the whole program without the other. I'd computed all the tables of every square number that was divisible into the sum of two other squares—"

"Whoa." Nick stopped him, putting up a hand. "Math was never my strong suit. Skip the details."

"Sorry," Larry said sheepishly. "When a project is your baby, you forget there are people out there who don't see it that way."

Nick bit his lip. He knew the feeling. Right

now the only baby he was interested in was his own. Jessica Wakefield.

"Anyway," Larry went on. "The point is that we're this close." He held his thumb and index finger a fraction of an inch apart. "There's no way he wouldn't show up to finish the project. For love or money. Except that this guy was definitely lovesick."

Nick's ears perked up. "What do you mean?"

Larry made a face as if he were smelling something rotten. "He used to come in reeking of this sickly sweet perfume. I finally had to ask him to leave his coat outside. Also, for the past few days he could barely concentrate. All he did was moan about his new girlfriend."

Nick sat on the edge of his seat. *Celine,* he thought. *That describes her perfume to a tee.* And if the guy was having girl trouble, that fit the profile of Alex's mystery hot-line caller too. "That sounds like the guy I'm looking for," Nick said. He could feel the excitement of the chase building in his chest.

Larry nodded. "I thought there was something wrong. No one would abandon their project unless—"

"What's his name?" Nick demanded. He was running out of time.

Larry shrugged. "Jordan. But I don't know his last name. He's a tall, skinny guy."

"Jordan," Nick repeated. Another piece in the puzzle. Now all he had to do was find out where this Jordan lived. But with nothing to go on but a first name, doing that would take a miracle!

"Ohhh," Elizabeth groaned, slowly opening one swollen eyelid. Her head felt like the SVU football team had used it for punting practice. She pushed her tongue around her mouth, trying to dislodge the old sock it seemed someone had shoved in there. But all she managed to dislodge was an extreme case of sour breath. "Where am I?" she murmured.

The sheets pulled up to her chin were blue and white striped, not a pattern she owned.

Uh-oh. She sat up to look around the room, but the sudden movement sent a sharp pain through her head, blurring her vision and making her collapse back on the pillow. From where she lay all she could make out was the hazy outline of a dresser and a desk. She squinted, and a chair came into focus. On it were a pair of jeans and a yellow T-shirt, carefully folded.

They look just like my clothes, she thought. *Then what am I wearing?* She peeked under the covers to explore. The white T-shirt she had on reached down to her knees. It was huge—man size!

Oh no, she thought, her stomach twisting with dread. *Please tell me I'm not in some strange guy's bed.* She grimaced and closed her eyes, desperately trying to piece together the previous night.

"I went to the party with Alex and Noah—" she reminded herself shakily. The room had been crowded and she'd been hot and thirsty. She also remembered drinking the punch. But after that her memory was hazy. All she could recall was being in a dark corner with some loser slobbering all over her. Elizabeth shuddered and pulled the covers up tighter around her neck. A sick feeling spread through her body. *What am I going to do?* she thought.

Wincing anxiously, she explored the rest of the bed with her bare leg. Nothing but empty space. Thank goodness. Whoever owned that bed wasn't in it with her now. *I've got to get out of here!*

Elizabeth's eyes searched frantically for the owner of the room. Her vision locked on a large poster of a man who seemed to be soaring through the air. There was a basketball in his palm.

"I know who that is," Elizabeth whispered. "That's Michael Jordan. Air Jordan." *Todd has that poster in his room.*

"Of course," she murmured with relief as the

rest of the previous evening's events fell into place. "Todd saved me last night. I'm in Todd's bed. Todd's bed?" she cried. This time she shot up and stayed there, forgetting the pounding in her head. *Did Todd take advantage of me while I was drunk?*

Elizabeth flung off her covers, ready to jump out of the bed and furiously face him. But he wasn't there.

A deep breathing sound cut through the silence of the room. Elizabeth followed the sound, scooting to the foot of the bed. On the floor below her Todd was lying on his side, a lock of his brown hair curled on his brow. His broad bare shoulder peeked out from under an old blanket. He was fast asleep.

Elizabeth felt her anger lessen. "Todd looks like an angel." She sighed, an excited shiver making its way up her spine. She watched as he shifted onto his back and the blanket fell to expose the tops of his strong arms and muscular chest. He looked incredibly sexy, and Elizabeth couldn't help but gaze at him with a smile on her face.

I spent the night—alone—with Todd, she thought, her eyes sparkling. Suddenly she swallowed hard, her face blushing furiously. But what else had happened?

*   *   *

"Here goes," Celine murmured to herself as she walked across the marbled entrance of the Sweet Valley Savings & Loan. The doors of the bank had been thrown open moments before at precisely eight A.M. Celine forced herself to walk with studied care. No use hurrying or acting nervous—that would only bring attention to herself. And since she was attempting to defraud the bank, attention was the last thing she wanted.

She clutched Lila's bank card between her gloved fingers and made a point of turning away from the security cameras. Even though she'd wrapped a large scarf around her hair so they couldn't tell she didn't have Lila's brunette mane and wore large, dark sunglasses to hide her eyes, she was nervous about being discovered.

Luckily she and Lila were about the same height and build. Nothing a pair of high heels couldn't correct.

Celine picked up a withdrawal slip from the counter. *Five thousand dollars,* she wrote out in a shaky hand. It took her three attempts before she felt the signature could fool even Lila herself. "It should," she whispered. "I practiced most of the night."

Now she was ready for the final challenge. Celine got on the shortest line and instantly regretted it. The teller who'd seemed so fast in dealing with customers was that way because she kept rejecting slips. "This is too messy for me to read," Celine heard her complain, sending a sad old man back to the counter to fill out another slip. When the next customer appeared at her window, the teller rolled her eyes. "You haven't brought the proper ID—go see the manager."

"Gracious!" Celine winced. "Lila's bank card better be enough ID for that old battle-ax or I'm sunk."

She adjusted her sunglasses and stepped up to the counter.

"And what can I do for you?" the teller snapped.

Celine nervously pushed Lila's bank card and the withdrawal slip across the Plexiglas divider.

The teller pulled at it with a growl and then her eyes shot up. "Miss Fowler!" she exclaimed, all smiles and flattery. "You didn't have to wait in line. Here, let me show you a seat." The teller ran out from behind her booth. "Mr. Jefferson," she called. "Miss Fowler is here."

A man in a pinstripe suit darted from behind his desk to pull out a chair. "Miss Fowler," he said, his voice full of delight. "How good to see you again. Please take a seat. How can we help you?"

Celine gave a little cough and pointed to her

throat. They certainly knew Lila didn't speak with a southern accent.

"Oh, Miss Fowler," the teller gushed. "I'm so sorry you have a sore throat." She elbowed Mr. Jefferson and gave him a significant look. "I'm sure Miss Fowler would like something to drink."

Mr. Jefferson was on his feet like a shot, pouring Celine a tall glass of water. "And let me just pull up your portfolio on the screen." He happily studied the figures that flashed before them. "Yes, yes, your stock in the Peruvian gold mine has doubled again. But I won't bore you with those little details. What can I do for you today?"

Celine pointed to her throat again and shrugged.

"Mr. Jefferson," the teller admonished. "Here is Miss Fowler's withdrawal slip."

"Of course," Mr. Jefferson gasped, jumping up again. He looked at the slip that the teller handed him and rushed off toward the vault.

Celine leaned back in the soft leather client chair and smiled. *This is easier than taking candy from a baby,* she thought smugly. Maybe she'd keep Lila's bank card for a day or two. If five thousand dollars was this easy, how hard would an additional ten thousand be?

Celine looked up as Mr. Jefferson returned

with a thick bundle of one hundred dollar bills and a very distinguished-looking gentleman in an expensive three-piece suit. *He must be the bank manager,* she thought, smiling and holding out her hand. *Obviously another person to fawn over me. I could get used to this.* Celine licked her lips as she took possession of the money.

The man looked at her blankly and turned to Mr. Jefferson. "I thought you said my daughter was here. This young woman isn't Lila."

"What?" Mr. Jefferson and the bank teller gasped.

Celine leaped to her feet. "Oh, lordy, out of my way," she screamed as she rushed to the front door.

"Stop, thief!" Mr. Jefferson hollered after her. "Stop that woman!"

Elizabeth got up quietly from Todd's bed and quickly changed back into her own clothes. She tiptoed silently across the room, her hand inches shy of the doorknob when Todd sat up.

"Liz," he called. "Wait."

Elizabeth felt her face flush an embarrassed pink as she turned to meet his eyes. "I'm, uh . . . sorry," she stuttered, "for anything I did last night. I can't remember much." She flinched. She was desperate to know if anything had happened between them, but she didn't dare ask him.

Todd laughed and ran a hand through his hair. "Don't worry. I've seen a lot worse. I've *done* a lot worse." He started to stand up. "I have something for you."

Elizabeth took a deep breath as the blanket covering Todd's body slowly slid down, exposing more of his firm, golden skin. A tingle starting to race from the top of her head to her toes as she wondered if under the blanket he was—

Todd took a step toward her, the blanket falling to his feet.

—*covered*, Elizabeth thought with relief. The lower half of his body was clothed in a baggy pair of blue sweatpants.

Todd walked past her and opened the top drawer of his desk. Elizabeth watched his powerful back muscles move as he rummaged through it. Then he turned with a smile on his face. "This is for good luck. Close your eyes and give me your hand."

Elizabeth shut her eyes tightly and held out her arm. *He's going to pull me toward him,* she thought, her knees beginning to shake. She quickly wet her lips, waiting for his warm mouth.

Todd touched her hand. "Keep your eyes closed," he warned.

Elizabeth squeezed them hard and pursed her lips ever so slightly.

His hand grasped hers, and she felt something soft being slipped over her fingers. "You can open them now."

Elizabeth looked down. On her wrist was a scruffy white sweatband with a red stripe.

"It's my good-luck sweatband." Todd grinned. "I wear it every time I play. And each time I've worn it to an exam this semester, I've gotten an A. I'm hoping some of the luck can rub off in the courtroom to help Jess."

Elizabeth stared down at the sweatband, feeling slightly confused. She'd been sure he was going to kiss her. Did that mean they did . . . or they *didn't* last night? She had to know. "Todd," she asked shakily, her heart pounding wildly in her chest. "Did I . . . did we—"

Todd cocked his head, a faint smile playing at the edges of his lips. He shook his head. "You were drunk. I would never take advantage of you in that state."

Elizabeth stifled a sigh of relief and gazed into Todd's twinkling brown eyes. *I'm not drunk now,* flashed across her mind. *Maybe now Todd will kiss me.*

Todd turned away to grab a sweatshirt. "So when is the hearing?"

Elizabeth swallowed hard as she stared at his

back, surprised at the disappointment she felt rising within her. "Nine o'clock," she blurted.

"You'd better get going," Todd advised. "It's almost eight-thirty now."

Elizabeth gasped. "I won't have a chance to shower and change. I'll have to go to court like this." She rushed for the door but hesitated when she reached it and turned toward him. For the life of her she couldn't remember why she and Todd ever broke up. "Thanks for everything," she murmured gratefully, gazing one last time into his eyes. "For saving me last night. And for this lucky sweatband."

Chapter
Eleven

_____

Nick leaned back dejectedly at Larry's PC terminal in the engineering computer lab. "Now what?" he complained. "I'm not going to get very far with only a first name."

Larry scratched the top of his red head. "Even if you could get the registrar to give you a list of engineering students, it'd be at least a couple hundred names. I personally know three Jordans in the department, and I've only been here six months. Do you know anything else about him?"

Nick twisted in his seat. "I know he comes from a town somewhere along the coast, but I don't see how that's going to help." Even if he had the proper resources, finding Jordan was going to be a big job. *And*, he reminded himself, *I'm not a police officer anymore. Nobody at the department is going to help me now.*

Larry sat up a little straighter. "That's getting somewhere. We know his name, his department, and a general location of where he's from. Jules is your man."

Nick frowned. "Who's Jules?"

Larry grimaced and pointed to the group of guys who had been giving Nick a hard time earlier. "He's one of them."

Nick winced. "Not them. How could they help? They can't even speak properly."

Larry laughed. "I know, but Jules wrote a brilliant cluster analysis program. He was able to take three disparate conditions and combine them to show an outcome of—"

Nick threw up his hands. "Please, keep it simple."

Larry gave him an understanding smile. "OK. Jules's program can take information and cross-reference it against everyone else in the department. He can give us a list of all engineering students named Jordan who live along the coast."

"Really?" Nick asked, feeling excitement rise in him. "Let's go talk to Jules, then."

Nick followed Larry over to the laughing, rowdy group he'd talked to earlier.

"Jules, we need your help," Larry said. "The detective here needs to do a cluster analysis to locate an engineering student named Jordan."

Nick had hoped Jules was one of the quieter ones. Maybe the tall, skinny kid who'd stood off to one side of the gang or the short, dark-haired one who'd only laughed along with the others. *Anyone but him,* Nick thought, his heart sinking as the wiry guy turned to him with a big grin across his face.

"Cluster analysis," Jules crowed. "Press any key to continue."

Nick groaned and turned to Larry. "Can you interpret, please."

Larry laughed. "Sure. That means Jules is willing to help."

The group made room for Larry and Nick, who sat down on either side of Jules in front of a nearby PC.

"What's the first datum, dude?" Jules asked.

Nick frowned. "What?"

"What information do you have?" Larry interpreted.

"First name, Jordan. Engineering student. Family's house estimated thirty miles north or south of SVU campus on the coast."

Jules nodded, and his fingers flew across the keyboard. "We'll need to interface and download with the main CPU to extract the relative bytes for forecasting. That access is prohibited through normal binary channels."

Nick closed his eyes. He wasn't even going to try and make sense of that.

"What he's saying," Larry explained, "is that he's going to have to break into the SVU registrar's system."

Nick's eyes shot open. "Can he do that?"

Larry shook his head. "That's not Jules's specialty, but the other guys can. Calvin, Matty, we need to access the registrar's files."

The heavyset guy grinned and leaned over Nick's chair. "Matty, at your service."

Nick groaned. *The other troublemaker,* he thought.

Matty tapped his fingers on his plump face. "The registrar's office has a security code. We'll have to run a program that can bypass the system."

"But keep it clean," a guy with thick glasses piped up. "The last time you hacked the president's files, we had campus security on our tails."

Matty blushed. "Minor quirk. I can get in through a back door between timed backups."

"Do it," Jules said, pounding away on his keyboard. "I've got the cluster analysis program set up and primed for data. I need the information downloaded to run this baby."

Matty slid in between Nick and Jules and began typing in code. To Nick, it looked like a lot of gibberish. Symbols and icons flashed across the screen. But suddenly something seemed to explode as strings of binary code, all zeros and ones, scrolled across the screen. After a few moments the monitor blinked and was still again.

"There's your data, Dr. J," Matty said. "Cluster time."

Jules slid back in front of the keyboard and executed a few strokes. This pulled a complicated formula onto the screen. He tapped furiously at the keyboard, and then the icons and symbols disappeared, replaced by a revolving head. The face on it had Jules's features.

Jules looked over at Nick and grinned. "Won't be long now. The computer's thinking."

From across the room a printer started to sputter and hum. Jules, Matty, Larry, and the rest of the guys jumped up and ran over to it. "Come on," Larry called to Nick. "Here's your answer."

Jules ripped the sheet from the computer printer and laughed. "Excellent! I knew the cross-checking subroutine would work." He passed the sheet to Nick.

On it were two names and addresses. Jordan Andrews in Port Calahan and Jordan Wilson in Santa Lucia.

"Thanks, guys," Nick enthused. "This is great." Now all he had to do was find the right

Jordan and get to the bottom of the drug deal before the judge and grand jury rendered their decision in Jessica's indictment hearing. He'd have to hurry. In a thirty-mile radius from SVU, Port Calahan and Santa Lucia couldn't be farther apart.

"Next time I need computer assistance in tracking down a dangerous criminal, you're the guys I'll come to."

The students laughed and waved him on. "Good luck."

"And thanks, Larry," Nick called from the door. "I owe you one."

"I'll remember that," Larry called back, "next time I get a parking ticket."

"Oyez, oyez," cried the bailiff as Jessica was led into the grand jury hearing. "The case of the *People of the State of California versus Jessica Wakefield* is now called. The Honorable Judge Dodd presiding."

Jessica took a deep breath. "Be brave," she murmured to herself. "The truth will come out and then this will all be over."

All heads turned to watch her approach the bench. Elizabeth, Steven, and Billie peered at her from the front row. Behind them were Alex, Noah, Isabella, Lila, and a score of her Theta sisters. *My friends have come out in force for me,* she thought. But where was Nick? Her eyes darted around the courtroom for him. "Liz said he was going to help me," she whispered to herself, feeling panic rising in her chest. "Why isn't he here? Doesn't he care enough to come to my trial?"

Jessica took a deep breath, trying to steady her nerves, and then turned as she attempted a smile for her actual supporters. But as she started to make eye contact, she realized with a start that each and every one of their faces was drawn and anxious. *They haven't found anything to clear my name,* she thought. *That's why they look worried. They know I'm cooked!*

Jessica could feel tears burning behind her eyes. Her bottom lip trembled and a sob fought to escape from her chest. She swallowed it down, twisting the hem of Elizabeth's linen jacket in her hand.

"Stay strong, Jess," she whispered. "Remember what Mr. Mills told you." Too much emotion in the courtroom was bad. The jury would be watching her and might interpret her tears as an admission of guilt.

Jessica couldn't let that happen. She straightened herself up and took her seat at the defendant's table, recalling her fortitude from the previous night. *I will overcome,* she thought. *And even if they convict me wrongly for a crime*

I didn't mean to commit, I'll keep my dignity.
She smoothed down her skirt and looked straight ahead.

Mr. Mills shuffled through his papers beside her and chewed on his lip. "I hope that's just hunger, not nervousness," Jessica whispered to herself. "Or I'm in bigger trouble than I thought." The courtroom was smaller and quieter than yesterday's room. The big difference was the twelve grand jurors seated on one side of Judge Dodd's large mahogany bench.

Jessica gulped. "I hope those grand jurors know a person is innocent until proven guilty," she whispered. *Not like Nick,* she thought, wincing.

"Don't worry about that, Jessica," Mr. Mills responded. "The jury has been briefed on their duties. They know the law."

Judge Dodd banged his gavel. "Jessica Wakefield will now rise."

Jessica and Mr. Mills stood before the judge.

"I won't waste time with preliminaries," the judge stated solemnly. "I've convened this special public grand jury hearing to determine if you should face trial and possible conviction on the charges that the bailiff is about to read."

The bailiff stepped forward, holding a sheet of paper. "Jessica Wakefield," he read, "you have been charged with possession of cocaine with the intent to distribute. How do you plead?"

Jessica turned to face the jury. She raised her chin and threw back her shoulders. "Not guilty," she replied in a loud, clear voice.

"This hearing will now commence," the judge declared.

The district attorney from her bail hearing smoothly appeared at her elbow. Today he was wearing a charcoal gray suit and a red silk tie. With a smug nod, he motioned for Jessica to sit down.

Jessica narrowed her eyes, waiting until Mr. Mills took her by the arm and led her to her seat. She refused to be bullied by the prosecution.

"Your Honor," the district attorney began. "I'd like to call Detective Rogers to the stand."

Jessica closed her eyes as the story of the evening of her arrest was recounted by the police officer. "We apprehended Ms. Wakefield in the parking lot outside the SVU science building at approximately seven-thirteen P.M. In her possession at that time was a package containing a hundred grams of cocaine."

"Objection, Your Honor," Mr. Mills interrupted, rising to his feet. "Unless the witness had a scale in his pocket, the amount of cocaine in the package is pure conjecture."

"Sustained," Judge Dodd replied.

The police officer rolled his eyes. "There was a significant amount of cocaine in the package. Subsequent laboratory analysis showed its weight to be one hundred grams."

The district attorney leaned against the bench before the jurors. "A significant amount of cocaine," he repeated, nodding to them. "More than what a person would need for their own use?"

"Oh, for sure," the police detective agreed. "The quantity the defendant was carrying would keep a small army high for a month."

The district attorney gave a slippery smile. "So you would agree, Detective Rogers, that the amount Ms. Wakefield had in her possession would not be for her sole use but more likely for sale to other drug users?"

"Objection," Mr. Mills claimed. "Counsel is leading the witness."

"Objection overruled," Judge Dodd replied, banging his gavel. "The prosecution is obviously seeking an opinion."

Mr. Mills sat down with a heavy sigh. Jessica cringed. That didn't seem like a very good sign.

Detective Rogers gave an insolent smile. "That's correct," he stated. "In my opinion, that is."

Jessica leaned over to Mr. Mills. "What are they getting at?" she asked. "What difference does it make how much I was carrying?"

Mr. Mills turned his head toward her. "They're trying to keep us from arguing that you had the drugs for personal use and not for sale. While personal possession is still a crime, it's not as bad as intending to distribute drugs for a profit."

"Oh no," Jessica cried. "So they're trying to throw the book at me?"

Mr. Mills nodded sadly. "I'm afraid so. But losing that debate hasn't lost our case." He patted her hand nervously. "Everyone loses a few arguments."

A few arguments! Jessica thought wildly. The way those jury members were glaring at her, she was sure they'd already made up their minds. One more point won by the opposing counsel and she was as good as sentenced.

"Anyone home?" Nick yelled as he pounded his fist on the front door of the Andrews' house. It was the home of the first Jordan on his list. He took a step back and stared up at the white clapboard facade. Its drawn curtains made it look closed up. But there was a car in the driveway and the morning newspaper was still on the mat. To Nick's detective eye, that meant someone was home.

A neighbor from next door stepped out onto her porch in a housedress and curlers. "Are you the police?"

Nick nodded. "Just a routine call, ma'am." There was no reason to get the neighborhood in an uproar.

The woman crossed her arms and nodded knowingly. "He's up all night, that one," she complained. "Playing that loud rock music the kids like these days. It's a wonder he has any hearing left at all."

"Then he's home?" Nick asked.

"Oh yes, he's in there. Sleeping. You can be sure of that. He was such a good boy when he was young."

Nick smiled. "Thanks, ma'am." That sounded like his man. If the guy was up every night partying, that fit the profile of a cocaine user.

"Just doing my neighborly duty. My name's Mrs. Peabody, and I keep an eye on things going on around this block. That boy is a real heartbreak to his parents. They wanted him to—"

"Thank you, ma'am," Nick cut in. "I'll take it from here." Nick banged on the door again.

Finally the front door creaked open and a sleepy-looking guy in red-and-white polka-dot pajamas looked blankly at Nick. He was tall and skinny, and Nick felt an excited flutter in his stomach. This could be his man.

"Yes?" the guy asked, wiping sleep from his eyes.

Since Nick no longer had his badge, he

flashed his library card quickly. "I'm Detective Nick Fox. Are you Jordan Andrews?"

The young man nodded.

"I'd like to ask you a few questions, Mr. Andrews. May I come in?"

"Sure," Jordan said, stepping back to let Nick enter the living room. "What's this all about?"

Nick surveyed the scene for any possible accomplices. The room was small and stuffy, crammed full of furniture and dominated by a huge television set. "I'm asking the questions," Nick replied. "Are you a student at SVU in the engineering department?"

Jordan's face colored, and he started to stutter. "How did you know? How did you find me?"

Nick could feel the hairs on the back of his neck stand up. This guy was about to come clean. He knew the symptoms. "Your colleagues had a hand in that."

Jordan's bottom lip began to quiver. He slumped down into a leather easy chair. "It was Jules, wasn't it? He and Matty sent you here."

Nick walked in front of Jordan, towering over him. "That's not relevant, Mr. Andrews," he informed him. "Let's stick to the point." The last thing Nick wanted was this guy going after the engineering students who'd turned him in.

"Do you want to tell me about it here or down-town?"

Jordan dropped his head in his hands. "I was never good enough," he sobbed. "All I ever wanted to be was an engineer. All through high school I never went out. I only studied."

Get on with it, Nick urged in his mind. *Criminals always have their excuses.*

"Then I got to SVU and there were all these women."

"Like Celine?" Nick prompted. All Alex's evidence against Celine was totally circumstantial. Nick's only hope was to get a confession from Jordan and convince him to testify against her.

Jordan shrugged. "And Nina and Angela and Sharon."

Nick frowned. *Who were they and were they all involved?* Nick pulled his notebook from the pocket of his leather jacket. "I'll need a list of names and addresses."

Jordan looked up and blinked. "I don't know that. Those girls wouldn't give me the time of day."

"But Celine did," Nick stated.

Jordan knitted his brow. "Celine? Who's she?"

Nick gritted his teeth. *This guy is more slippery than he looks.* "We know all about Celine, but we'll leave it for now. Tell me what happened behind the science building."

Jordan made a confused face, his eyes widening. "Science building?" He nervously rubbed his hands back and forth on the chair's arms. "What do you mean?"

Nick threw up his hands and started to pace in front of Jordan. "OK, tell it your way." He mentally kicked himself. He knew better than to lead a suspect during an interrogation. But he didn't have time to play games.

Jordan took a deep breath and drew his long, bony knees up under his chin. "I couldn't concentrate. I'd never been away from home before. Everyone else was going out at night. Jules and Matty. Even that redhead, Larry. I wanted to go out and have fun too. That was my mistake. Those guys were smart. They didn't need to study all the time. I did!"

Jordan leaped to his feet, and Nick took a step back, not sure how volatile this guy would get. Criminals could be dangerous when cornered, even when they were weak and skinny.

"I failed," Jordan cried. "I wasn't smart enough. I had to drop out of school," he finished with a sob, collapsing back into his chair.

Nick frowned. "So you're not at SVU anymore?"

Jordan shook his head without looking up. Nick gripped him by the arms. "Explain this to me. You live here and drive down to hang out on campus?"

Jordan looked up, his face molten from emotion and tears. "I don't go to campus. Not anymore. I could never show my face there again. I failed. I—"

Nick let go of Jordan. "Wait," he cut in, putting up his hand. "Then where were you on Tuesday night?"

Jordan screwed up his face. "Here. Like I always am. Probably watching TV with my parents."

Nick frowned. *At home with his parents watching TV?* he thought with a sinking feeling. *This new profile doesn't sound right at all!* "But this loud music you play and staying up all night—"

Jordan shook his head. "That was one night. Tuesday, actually. My parents were out at bingo. But please don't tell them."

Nick took a step closer to Jordan. "Tell them what? That you took their car and went to campus?" Maybe he was on the right track after all.

Jordan flushed bright red. "No. I told you, I don't go there. I was here listening to music. It wasn't loud, I swear. But Mrs. Peabody complained. She complains about everything. She sent the cops over and they made me turn it off. My parents will kill me if they find out."

Nick made a face. The feeling in his gut was getting worse and worse. "What time was this?"

"Seven P.M. Not even that late."

Nick groaned and ran a hand over his face. Seven P.M. and the cops came! That meant this Jordan had an airtight alibi for Tuesday night. *I'm wasting my time on the wrong guy!* Nick thought as he headed for the door.

"Wait," Jordan called. "Don't you want to hear the rest of my story? How Jules and Matty played those practical jokes on me?"

Nick shook his head and bolted down the driveway to his car. At this point even if he found the *right* Jordan, he'd never get back to Sweet Valley and Jessica's indictment hearing on time.

Chapter Twelve

Celine looked around the courtroom and gave her honey blond curls a satisfied toss. Her heartbeat seemed to be back to normal after her narrow escape from the bank earlier that morning. Those guards might still be chasing her if she hadn't finally lost them in the Sweet Valley Mall.

"Thank goodness for shopping centers," she whispered to herself with a sigh. With a wad of crisp one hundred dollar bills in her purse, her robbery clothes safely disposed of in a convenient Dumpster, and an appointment with Scarface and his cronies for later that day, she could finally relax and indulge herself. And watching Jessica's downfall was by far the most pleasing activity she could think of.

Celine sighed deeply. "My luck has certainly turned around," she murmured. "And I've got a ringside view of the proceedings." What a circus it was too. All Jessica's friends and family were fit to be tied. Miss Priss, Elizabeth Wakefield, looked like something a bomb had fallen on. Judging by the whiff Celine had gotten when she'd breezed past her in the corridor, Elizabeth had been hitting the bottle a little too hard.

"Too bad, so sad," Celine whispered in a singsong voice. "Not only is this *dreadful* trial going to ruin Jessica Wakefield, but it's brought her sister, Miss High-and-Mighty, down to earth as well!"

The district attorney approached the witness box. "Now, Detective Rogers, you've already told us about the cocaine found in Ms. Wakefield's possession. Tell me, do you have any reason to believe that she had an accomplice in the drug transaction?"

Celine watched him and pouted her lips seductively. "Such a handsome district attorney," she purred to herself. "And clever too. He's got Jessica's lawyer tied up in ribbons." Which was going to leave Jessica gift wrapped for a full-blown trial.

Celine flicked a piece of dust from her immaculate white linen suit and adjusted the exquisite white hat that was perched atop her head. She'd barely had time enough to run home and change before the trial started. She could feel Lila and Alex's eyes boring into her from across the room. She glanced over at them and tapped the brim of her hat. *Don't mind me, girls,* she thought, putting on her most innocent smile. *I'm just another Theta sister, here to support poor Jessica.*

Lila bent her head and started whispering frantically to Alex.

"Oh my," Celine murmured as they both looked up and scowled at her. "If their eyes were daggers, I'd be positively full of holes by now!" Celine laughed and moistened her lips. Now what could they be gabbing about? She'd announced at the Theta party she'd be at the trial. And there was no way Lila could know about that clever little bank card scam. *Maybe it's my hat,* she thought. Too festive for them? It certainly was what they were staring at.

Celine smiled with glee. *It is audacious of me to wear this gorgeous hat to Jessica's hearing,* she thought. But why shouldn't she wear it? The hat was rightfully hers, wasn't it? The hat *and* the pleasure of watching Jessica Wakefield take the fall for that drug deal.

The district attorney's voice rose loudly as he made his next point, cutting into Celine's thoughts. "So Detective Rogers, after you arrested Ms. Wakefield and made a thorough search of the environs, you found no one else present? No *mystery man* that the public defender is trying to conjure up? Is that correct?"

"Objection!"

Celine laughed as Jessica's frumpy lawyer stumbled to his feet. The man's shirt had pulled loose from his wrinkled pants and his bow tie was practically unraveled.

"Poor Jessica." Celine smirked. "Doesn't she know appearance is nine-tenths of the law?"

"Objection overruled," the judge growled. "Sit down, Mr. Mills, and stop trying to upset these proceedings."

"But Your Honor—" Mr. Mills pleaded.

"I said sit down!" The judge banged his gavel with such force, Celine jumped.

Now that's one man I wouldn't want on my bad side, Celine thought. *He looks like Granny Boudreaux—without her wig on!*

Celine leaned back on the bench and fluttered her eyelashes smugly, prepared to watch the gorgeous district attorney hammer the final nails into Jessica Wakefield's coffin.

Nick slammed on the brakes of his black Camaro, screeching to a halt outside Jordan Wilson's house in Santa Lucia, and leaped from the car. The front door opened as Nick raced up the paved walkway. A tall, skinny young man peered out at him.

"Police!" Nick shouted, reaching for his library card. The young man tried to slam the door, but Nick stopped it with his foot. The guy jumped back with a cry, and Nick pushed his way in, toppling him backward onto a plaid couch. "Are you Jordan Wilson?" Nick bellowed.

"I might be," the guy jabbered. "I have to leave. I have to go meet my parents. They're expecting me in town."

Nick stood over him, barely able to contain his wrath. There was no time to lose. "Is your name Jordan Wilson?"

Jordan nodded meekly. "You've got the wrong guy. I didn't do anything. I swear, whatever you think I did, it's all a mistake. I'm innocent."

"Stop babbling," Nick barked. "Where were you on Tuesday night? Seven P.M.?"

Jordan shuddered, wrapping his gangly arms around his shoulders. "I don't know where I was. I was out. I was not anywhere that I wasn't supposed to be."

Nick narrowed his eyes. "You were behind the science building, weren't you?"

"No, no," Jordan cried. "Not there. I was way across campus from there."

Nick gritted his teeth. Jessica's indictment hearing had already started. He needed answers now! "I know you're lying, Jordan," he shouted. "You showed up at the meeting place behind the science building with a package containing a hundred grams of cocaine. Now tell me what happened."

Jordan gripped the edge of the couch, his knuckles turning as pale as his short white blond hair. "No!" he screamed. "It wasn't me. I swear. I was never there. I hate science. I go out of my way to avoid that building."

Nick hovered over Jordan, his arms shaking in anger. "Stop lying. We have a witness."

Jordan blanched. "Who? Jessica Wakefield? The girl with the drugs."

Nick grabbed Jordan by the front of his Lakers sweatshirt. "I didn't say a name," he hissed. "And how do you know she had drugs?"

Jordan gulped. "I . . . I heard it on the radio."

Nick pulled him closer until they were nose to nose. "The arrest was never broadcast, Jordan," he said in his most menacing voice. "The only people who know that information are the police and the guy who was there."

Jordan started to shake. "Her friends know. It's all over campus." He laughed nervously. "That's how I know. Idle gossip."

Nick let go of Jordan, and he fell back down onto the couch. Nick started to pace. He'd get the truth out of this liar if it was the last thing he did. Jessica's arrest *was* known all over campus, but his sixth sense told him Jordan knew about it because he'd been involved. Now Nick just had to get him to admit it.

"Why would Jessica Wakefield point you out, Jordan?" he demanded. "She described you to a tee. Even the SVU Engineering sweatshirt you wear so often."

Jordan flushed and his pale blue eyes flew down to his sweatshirt, then back up to Nick.

"What's the matter, Jordan?" Nick goaded him. "Forget what you put on every morning?"

Jordan shook his head. "I never had a sweatshirt that said SVU Engineering. It must be some other engineering student."

Nick sneered. "That's an easy enough thing to check. I'm sure your mother will know."

Jordan's eyes widened. "OK, maybe I do. But that doesn't mean I was behind the science building."

Nick turned away. Jordan had a point. The only witness was Jessica, and she was up on drug charges. Her word wouldn't be worth much against his. Nick would have to try something else. He turned back and grabbed Jordan's foot.

"*Nike,*" he cried with a sly smile. He ripped the sneaker from Jordan's foot. "Size ten!"

Jordan's face paled. "What are you getting at?"

Nick snorted. "The gardener watered the grass there Tuesday afternoon," he said with a laugh, quickly improvising. "Only a few hours before you and Ms. Wakefield met. You left sneaker prints all over the area. Five minutes with the lab boys downtown and we'll have indisputable proof you were there." Nick tossed the sneaker back at Jordan in triumph.

Jordan bit his lip, hugging the sneaker to his chest. "OK, OK. I was there. But I know nothing about any package. I know nothing about anything. I was there by mistake. I got lost. I made the wrong turn."

Nick sneered. "I don't care about your excuses, Jordan. I want the facts and I want them now. Do you admit to carrying a package and exchanging it with Jessica Wakefield?"

Jordan frantically shook his head. "No. I wasn't carrying any package. Someone must have dropped it. I picked it up and Jessica said it was hers. Then I handed it over."

Nick sighed. "Jordan, Jordan, Jordan. You're not making this easy on yourself."

"I swear that's the truth."

Nick hovered above him. "Then why did you deny being there?"

Jordan pressed back hard against the couch. "I didn't want to get involved," he whined. "Why should I bring trouble on myself?"

"What did Ms. Wakefield give you in return?"

Jordan shook his head furiously. "Nothing, I swear," he cried. "I wasn't part of any exchange."

Nick leaned so close to Jordan, they were breathing the same air. This question was vital. If Jessica gave Jordan money, then her whole defense would fall to pieces. It would mean she knew she was buying drugs. The prosecution would prove she intended to sell them to Nick. "I know you got something," he hissed. "If you don't start telling me the truth right now, I'm going to bring the law down on you so hard, it'll feel like a ton of bricks. I'm going to ask you once again. What did you get in exchange for the package?"

Jordan had pushed himself so far into the couch that the pillows were threatening to swallow him up. "A hatbox," he whispered. "With a floppy white hat in it."

Nick stepped back and swallowed. "Just a hatbox?" Nick demanded. "Don't tell me you gave up that valuable package without getting any money for it."

Jordan gulped, shaking his head and looking up at Nick imploringly. "There was no money. I swear. There was just the hat."

Nick turned away, closing his eyes for a

moment in thanks before turning back to continue his interrogation. "Why did you do it, Jordan? Who set you up?" Now he wanted the real culprit behind the drug deal.

Jordan's face crumpled. "I didn't mean to do anything wrong," he cried. "I didn't know what I was getting into. My girlfriend said it was documents. I never would have—"

"The girlfriend, Jordan," Nick cut in. "What's her name?"

Jordan covered his face with his hands. "I can't tell you that. I'll be killed!" he sobbed. "She'll tell the thugs she got the drugs from that I owe them the money and they'll kill me! They'll kill me!"

Nick tore Jordan's hands away from his face and shook him. "Get a grip. Would you rather spend years in jail to protect this girl? She betrayed you. She set you up." Nick let go of him.

Jordan caved, curling into a ball on the sofa. "Celine Boudreaux. She made me do it."

Elizabeth leaned forward in her seat in the courtroom behind Jessica and squeezed her sister's shoulder. "Don't worry, Jess," she whispered. "We're all here to support you. Mr. Mills will prove to the jury you're innocent."

Jessica turned and patted Elizabeth's hand.

"Thanks, Liz." She wrinkled her nose. "Whew! Have you been drinking?"

Elizabeth blushed and smoothed back her hair. *Is it that noticeable?* she thought. She tried to smooth the creases out of her T-shirt.

Jessica's eyes widened. "Liz, you look terrible. And you're wearing jeans. Are you hung over? What happened? Is it because of me?"

Elizabeth shook her head and gave her sister a weak smile. "No, don't worry. It's a long story." She wasn't even sure if she understood it. "I'll tell you all about it later—when we take you home after the hearing."

Jessica made a face. "*If* you take me home after the hearing. You might have to tell me from behind a wall of Plexiglas."

Elizabeth bit her bottom lip. "Don't think that way, Jess. I'm sure this will be over soon."

Mr. Mills stood and approached the jury. Jessica turned around to watch him, and Elizabeth crossed her arms, sitting back on the bench to listen. *Please, Mr. Mills,* she thought. *Get my sister out of this mess!*

"Ladies and gentlemen of the jury," Mr. Mills started, pacing in front of the jury box. "There has been a great deal of talk this morning about the time of the meeting and the amount of cocaine found in the package Ms. Wakefield was carrying. I want to make it perfectly clear that we are not disputing any of these facts. Jessica Wakefield *was* behind the science building at seven P.M. and *was* holding the package containing cocaine." He hesitated, his back now to the jury, letting them take in the full implication of his statement.

Elizabeth watched as the jury shifted in their seats, their faces flushed with interest. The room began to buzz.

"But!" Mr. Mills proclaimed loudly, twirling around and slamming his fist down on the jury box with a bang. "The other fact of the matter is that Jessica Wakefield had *no* idea what was in that package." Mr. Mills straightened and held up his fist. "Fact," he told them, raising his index finger. "Jessica Wakefield was in love with a man. A very mysterious man. A man who, it turns out, is the undercover cop who set up the drug deal." He raised two fingers. "Fact. She showed up at a meeting behind the science building in this man's place, hoping to learn the truth about him. My client believed this 'package' would contain secret documents that would give her insight into this young man." He added his third finger to the other two. "Fact—"

"Your Honor," the district attorney cut in slickly, breaking Mr. Mills's hold on the jury. "Are we supposed to believe Ms. Wakefield's drug dealing was nothing more than a childish prank?"

Elizabeth winced as a couple of the jury members nodded skeptically. In the bright morning light of the courtroom it did sound highly implausible.

"Your Honor," Mr. Mills cried out. "I'm establishing my client's defense here, and I would appreciate it if I weren't interrupted."

The nasty old judge glared down at Mr. Mills, and Elizabeth shuddered. All day he'd done nothing but overrule his objections and glower in Jessica's direction. The chances of him taking Mr. Mills's side were slim.

The judge smiled thinly. "The district attorney was only pointing out the obvious, Mr. Mills. But I will respect your wishes." He turned to the district attorney. "Sir," he requested, smiling widely, "would you please be kind enough to refrain from interrupting Mr. Mills during his oration. I'm sure he can shoot himself in the foot just as easily without our help."

Elizabeth's mouth dropped open. *How dare he!* she thought. *Why waste time on a trial? Why doesn't that horrible judge sentence Jess and throw away the key right now!*

The district attorney chuckled and took his seat.

Elizabeth watched, her spirits sagging, as Mr. Mills mopped at his brow with a wrinkled handkerchief.

"As I was saying," Mr. Mills continued, his voice sounding a lot less confident. "Ms. Wakefield had no idea what she was getting into. She was an innocent in love, checking up on her boyfriend. It was her bad luck that he was an undercover detective in the middle of a sting operation."

"That's for sure," the district attorney sneered to himself, but certainly loud enough for the jury to hear.

Elizabeth groaned. This wasn't going well at all. Jessica was coming off sounding like an idiot. She herself could think of half a dozen ways to pick apart Jessica's defense, and she knew the truth! If Nick wouldn't support Jessica's story, they'd never get the jury to believe her. With a sinking feeling in her stomach, Elizabeth realized, *Jessica might be going to jail for a crime she didn't commit!*

"Move it!" Nick screamed, waving his hand and flashing his headlights at the cars blocking his way. He was trying to race up the coastal highway toward Sweet Valley. Beside him, in the passenger seat, Jordan Wilson was white as a ghost.

One car moved out of his lane and Nick punched the gas pedal, practically driving up the backside of the next car in front of him. Jordan yelped as Nick slammed on the brakes.

"Come on!" Nick shouted, feeling his temper rise to a boil. But what did he expect? It was a sure bet that none of these people were headed to a grand jury hearing with the only witness who could save the woman they loved.

"Get out of the way!" Nick howled. The blue Volvo in front of him was keeping to a leisurely pace in the fast lane. Nick leaned on his horn and flashed his brights, but the graying head in the Volvo didn't react. Nick gritted his teeth and swerved around the big blue car's right side, barely missing a truck that had been coming up on their blind side. A screech of brakes, a blaring horn, and Jordan's scream let Nick know it had been a close call.

"Where did you learn to drive?" Jordan cried, his pale blue eyes bulging in terror. "A demolition derby?"

Nick glowered. "Relax! When we scrape sides, then you can start worrying."

Jordan gulped and clutched the dashboard.

Nick continued to cut through traffic, weaving around cars as Jordan was flung from side to side with each new twist of the wheel.

Nick glanced at the clock on the dashboard. Nine forty-five. *I'm running out of time!* Nick thought with alarm. The lawyers would be starting their summations any minute. *I've got to get there fast or Jessica's finished!*

Nick gunned the engine and cut across two lanes of traffic to the far right shoulder. It was a totally illegal move, but as long as no cars had broken down on the side of the road, it would save them precious minutes.

The powerful Camaro raced along the gravel shoulder, flying past the other cars as if they were barely moving. Jordan covered his face with his hands, a low moan escaping his lips.

"Don't worry, Jordan." Nick scowled, keeping his eyes glued to the shoulder for obstructions. "I haven't crashed this baby yet."

Jordan simpered. "There's always a first time."

Uh-oh! An old tire was blocking the shoulder. Nick swerved sharply into traffic, forcing a semi-trailer into the center lane, its big diesel horn howling in protest. With a quick flip of the wheel, they were back on the shoulder, the Camaro powering ahead.

Now the exit for Sweet Valley was coming up fast. *But it's on the other side of the freeway!* Nick realized with a start. No time to lose! He checked his mirror and slowed down long enough to let the big semi blow past. Then he floored the Camaro and barreled across the two lanes of traffic to his left, making the exit with only inches to spare. The Camaro's tires squealed angrily as Nick sped around the spiraling exit ramp. With a glance in his rearview mirror, he could see they were leaving a trail of black rubber skid marks around the sharp curve.

Jordan was curled up in a whimpering ball in the passenger seat. "Slow down!" he shrieked. "You're going to get us killed and then I'll never testify."

Nick narrowed his eyes as the car shot into Sweet Valley. The traffic here in town wasn't much better than it was on the highway. "I'll get you there alive. You just tell the judge he's got the wrong girl or I'll make sure I'm the one who drives you home. And that trip will make this one look like a Sunday cruise!"

Jordan went back to covering his face with a cry.

Nick raced up Sweet Valley Boulevard toward the city buildings and the courthouse. He zoomed through yellow lights and swerved around parked cars. The Camaro made a screeching right turn onto the street where the courtroom stood. Suddenly, though, a huge garbage truck pulled out, blocking their way. Nick slammed on the brakes, stopping only inches short of the truck's rear bumper.

"Take it easy, pal," a voice said. Two guys in overalls climbed down from the truck and meandered over to a line of garbage cans in front of an office building.

"Let me through," Nick hollered, reaching for

his badge, but coming up with only his library card. He flashed that anyway, but the garbage men ignored him.

Nick leaned on his horn. "Police business!" he shouted. "Move it!" Still they ignored him.

Nick threw the car into reverse, ready to floor it. But a large delivery van was pulling up behind him. They were hopelessly wedged in!

"Come on." He grabbed Jordan by the arm and pulled him out of the car through the driver's side.

"What are you doing?" Jordan cried. "You can't leave your car in the middle of the road."

"Watch me," Nick shot back. He dragged Jordan behind him, sprinting toward the courthouse. He was this close. Nothing was going to keep him from saving Jessica now!

Chapter Thirteen

Jessica jumped as Judge Dodd slammed down his gavel, signaling the end of the lawyers' arguments.

"Ladies and gentlemen of the jury," his voice boomed from the large mahogany bench. "We've all heard the evidence. Now it is up to you to decide whether the defendant, Jessica Wakefield, should be acquitted of all charges or if we should proceed to a full trial."

Jessica brushed a strand of golden blond hair from her face and looked at the jurors expectantly. She tried to imagine what the twelve of them were thinking. Six were frowning, four were studying her intently, and two had their arms crossed. There was no way to tell.

Judge Dodd's voice started up again, sounding even more adamant than usual. "Before I send you off to make this decision, I think it would be a good idea if I summed up the more important aspects of the evidence you've heard."

Jessica's heart sank. *Oh no,* she thought. She and Mr. Mills had been holding their own up to now. Mr. Mills had done a pretty convincing job as he went on. From thinking she'd be convicted for sure, she'd started to feel a glimmer of optimism as the hearing had proceeded. At the end of Mr. Mills's summation she'd felt that her chances of acquittal were fifty-fifty. But if Judge Dodd stuck in his two cents, Jessica knew she'd be in trouble.

She turned to Mr. Mills. "Is he allowed to do that?"

Her lawyer nodded his head sadly. "In a grand jury hearing the judge has a lot of leeway. Let's hope he keeps his summary objective."

Jessica groaned. *If he doesn't,* she thought, *I'm doomed.*

Judge Dodd took a deep breath and turned his full attention to the jury.

"Jessica Wakefield was arrested with a large quantity of cocaine in her possession," he began. "She admits she was behind the science building at the time a drug deal had been arranged with an undercover detective. From that point, however, the prosecution's and the defense's stories part company. Miss Wakefield wants you to believe she overheard a conversation setting up the meeting and that she went to

214

the science building on some kind of lark."

As Judge Dodd continued, Jessica could feel her face burning. Judge Dodd was brushing her story aside as if it were a tissue of lies. Even if the jurors had come around to her side during the hearing, they were never going to stay there now. *It's unfair*, Jessica thought. *Where's Nick? If only he were here. He could show them by his support that it's the truth.*

Judge Dodd shook his head purposefully. "Drugs," he spat. "Drugs and drug dealing should *never* be taken lightly. Drugs are no laughing matter. They are not a subject for silly courtship games. Drugs ruin lives. They should be stamped out." Judge Dodd slammed his fist on his desk.

Jessica let out an involuntary cry as he fixed her with a furious look before turning back to the jury. "There is a war on in our great country." His voice rose thunderously. "And the drug dealers are the hit men. Their actions should *not* be taken lightly. It is our duty as citizens to see that all drugs and drug dealers are expelled from our campuses, kept from our children, destroyed, and locked away!"

Jessica gripped the sides of her chair with such force, her hands ached. *Judge Dodd is practically ordering the jury to find me guilty!* she thought. She could spend the next year on trial—and the next twelve to fifteen years in jail!

She turned around to her family in the row behind her, her eyes brimming with tears. "What am I going to do?" she whispered frantically. Elizabeth grasped her hand while Steven leaned forward, his face molten with anger. "We'll fight this all the way," he hissed. "This judge is prejudiced."

Jessica gulped. That still meant a trial. As she turned back she caught a glimpse of a familiar-looking white hat on the other side of the courtroom.

Hey, Jessica realized with a start. *That's Lila's hat!* The one that was in the hatbox she'd given to the guy behind the science building! But Lila was sitting behind Elizabeth and Steven. Who was wearing that hat? Suddenly one of the spectators sat back in his seat and Jessica's eyes met Celine Boudreaux's straight on.

Celine? Jessica thought, her mind racing furiously.

Celine smiled kittenishly at her, pursing her lips up in a big, phony kiss. Jessica felt her face flush an angry red as Celine waved a discreet good-bye at her.

"This doesn't look good at all," Tom murmured to himself as he watched the proceedings from the back of the courtroom. Based on the hard evidence presented by the district attorney, he wouldn't be surprised if Jessica was sentenced to the full fifteen years after trial.

Tom shifted in his seat and took a quick glance at the judge. He'd slipped in late and had been keeping his head down most of the time. The last thing he wanted was to be seen by Elizabeth.

"I'm only here out of journalistic interest," he assured himself. "I'm certainly not here because of Liz." Though even to his ears the words rang hollow.

He averted his gaze as Alex sought out his eyes. "Great," he grumbled. "Now she'll go blabbing to Liz that I was here." *Well, let her know,* he thought bitterly. *She should be grateful I'm here.* He could have been watching the Rams play the Steelers with his father and half brother and sister.

Jake had practically started crying when Tom had told his family he couldn't make the ball game. And Mr. Conroy had kept insisting he come until Tom had finally explained why he couldn't. It was all he could do to keep the whole family from canceling their plans and his father from joining him at the trial.

"What would Liz think about that?" he muttered. "My father showing up to support her sister." Even though Mr. Conroy knew that Elizabeth had accused him of sexual harassment.

Tom shook his head, feeling his anger at Elizabeth bubbling up all over again. No matter how powerfully he was drawn to her, no matter how much he desired to be back in her arms, the painful fact of Elizabeth's betrayal kept coming back, sharp as a knife.

"Ladies and gentlemen of the jury, you may now proceed to the jury room to discuss your decision," Judge Dodd announced, and banged his gavel.

Jessica closed her eyes. *This is it.* In a few moments she'd be free or she'd be on her way back to jail. Either way, it was obvious she'd never see Nick again. He'd already forgotten her. *But if I'm convicted,* she thought with a tremor. *How many years staring at the grungy walls of a cell will it take before I forget him?*

A large man with a walrus mustache stood up. "Your Honor, as jury foreman I wish to state that we the jury do not need to deliberate. The decision is unanimous and has been obvious from the beginning."

Jessica's mouth dropped open. They weren't even going to talk about it?

"Jessica Wakefield," Judge Dodd commanded. "Please stand and face the jury."

Jessica stood on shaking legs. Mr. Mills's steady hand was all that was keeping her from toppling over. *This is it,* she thought. *They're sentencing me to a trial. My life is over.*

The jury foreman cleared his throat. "Jessica Wakefield, we find you—"

Suddenly there was a huge commotion at the back of the courtroom.

"Wait!" a loud voice shouted.

Jessica spun around to see Nick bursting through the doors of the courtroom dragging a tall, skinny guy behind him. Her heart leaped in her chest. "It's Nick," she cried, grabbing Mr. Mills by the arm. "He's found the guy who gave me the package!"

"Jessica Wakefield is innocent!" Nick shouted. "She didn't do anything." The courtroom went wild, buzzing with excited voices.

Nick rushed down the aisle to where Celine was sitting. "She's responsible," he yelled. He grabbed Celine's arm as she struggled to get away. "Celine Boudreaux is your drug dealer, and I have the evidence to prove it! Set Jessica Wakefield free!"

The judge rapped his gavel furiously. "This court will come to order!" he bellowed. "Or I'll clear it out!" The courtroom immediately fell silent. The judge pointed a gnarled finger at Nick. "What's the meaning of this disruption?" he demanded.

OK, Nick thought. *This is it.* He'd put together the evidence he needed; now he had to make his case. Jessica's case.

Nick pulled the cowering Celine to her feet, spilling the contents of her pocketbook—

including a thick wad of hundred dollar bills—
to the floor. "What's this?" Nick asked, scoop-
ing up the money and pulling out a yellow slip
that was peeking out from among the bills. "Lila
Fowler," he read from the withdrawal slip.

"I'm Lila Fowler," a voice suddenly rang out.
Nick turned his head toward the defense table,
where Lila was now standing. "My bank card
has been missing for several days," she announced. "And this morning an unauthorized
withdrawal was made from my account."

"Bailiff," Nick barked. "Hold this woman."
He pushed Celine toward the bailiff. "And hold
this money, which may be evidence of felony
bank fraud." Nick heard the entire courtroom
gasp in amazement.

"Order! Order!" the judge shouted, banging
his gavel.

Nick turned, again grabbing Jordan's arm like
a vise, and dragged him toward the judge's bench.

"Your Honor," Nick declared. "My name is
Nick Fox. I'm the detective who arrested Jessica
Wakefield, but I have new evidence that proves
she's completely innocent. Furthermore, I know
who the real drug dealer is now."

The judge rose to his feet, his black robes
flowing regally behind him. "This court will
take a short recess while I review these new allegations." He banged his gavel.

The courtroom hummed excitedly as people began standing up and milling around the room. Nick noticed Celine pulling away from the bailiff in the confusion. "Your Honor," Nick whispered furiously, "the culprit is trying to get away."

Judge Dodd banged his gavel once more. "Everyone seated. No one leaves my courtroom. Bailiff," he instructed. "Be sure that young lady is kept in custody."

Nick relaxed as Celine was forced back into her seat, the bailiff's hand locked on her arm.

The judge turned back to Nick. "Step into my chamber, Detective Fox."

Nick followed the judge, dragging Jordan behind them. The judge's chamber was a large room, furnished in dark, polished wood. The bookcases that lined one wall were crammed with weighty law tomes.

"Sit," Judge Dodd commanded as he took his seat behind an immense wooden desk. "What's this all about?"

Nick pushed Jordan down into one of the leather chairs facing the judge's desk and sat in the other. "Your Honor," Nick began. "This is Jordan Wilson, the man who gave Jessica Wakefield the package that night at the science building."

Jordan squirmed in his seat. "I was set up,"

he spluttered. "I didn't know what was in that package."

"Oh," the judge sneered contemptuously. "Another person who didn't know what was in the package."

Nick turned and gave Jordan a warning look. There wasn't time for Jordan to sit there making excuses. Judge Dodd wasn't known for his patience.

"Jordan," Nick demanded harshly. "What did Ms. Wakefield say when you gave her the cocaine?"

Jordan chewed on his bottom lip and looked nervously around the judge's chamber.

"The truth, Jordan," Nick barked. He didn't need Jordan coming up with any cock-and-bull stories to try and clear his own name.

Jordan winced. "She said, 'Thanks, I'll make sure the consulate gets these documents.'"

Nick turned back to Judge Dodd. "You see, Your Honor, Jessica wasn't a drug dealer. She went to that meeting in my place, thinking she would find out what I was really about. My undercover work at SVU had required me to keep her in the dark about my real identity."

The judge narrowed his eyes and scratched the white tuft of hair on the top of his head. "And you, young man," he asked, turning to Jordan, "you were the drug dealer?"

Jordan gulped loudly and gripped the sides of the chair. "No." He swallowed. "My girlfriend—I mean, my *ex*-girlfriend—told me to deliver the package. She said her old friend Nick was a big environmentalist and that the package would prove that Hightower Pharmaceuticals was involved in animal testing. She set me up."

The judge shifted in his seat. "Didn't you get suspicious when Ms. Wakefield showed up?"

Jordan shrugged. "All I knew was I was supposed to go to the meeting place and exchange my package for theirs."

"And what did Miss Wakefield give you in return?" the judge asked. Nick sat forward in his seat, his shoulders tensing. This was the heart of Jessica's defense. Her fate was hanging on Jordan's every word now.

Jordan grimaced. "A hatbox with a floppy white hat inside."

The judge frowned, turning to Nick. "A hat?"

Nick nodded. "Not just a hat. The hat that Celine Boudreaux is wearing in your courtroom right now."

Jordan blanched. "Celine Boudreaux, Your Honor, my ex-girlfriend."

The judge shook his head. "Let me see if I have this straight." He looked at Nick. "Miss Wakefield showed up in your place for the drug exchange?"

"That's correct," Nick agreed. "But she didn't know there was going to be an exchange. When Jordan asked her for the package he was supposed to get in return for the drugs, Jessica gave him the only thing she was carrying. Her friend's hatbox that she'd picked up that afternoon as a favor."

Nick watched as Judge Dodd's face lost a little of its scowl. *He's coming around,* Nick thought. *The truth is finally dawning on him!*

The judge nodded slowly. "Ah," he murmured. "And that hat eventually traveled back to the real culprit. That's the young woman the bailiff is holding in the courtroom."

Nick smiled. "That's her. That hat is even more distinctive than the marked bills I would have used in the exchange."

The judge laughed, but then his face clouded a little. "Other than a hat, which a good lawyer could argue was a gift from Mr. Wilson, what proof do we have? Sounds to me as if Miss Boudreaux has cleverly stayed clear of any incriminating acts."

Jordan slumped in his chair. "So it's back to me," he whined. "But I didn't know anything either. I swear it."

Nick shook his head. "Wait a minute, Jordan. You said Celine owes the drug suppliers a lot of money. I just confiscated the money on her person, and the withdrawal slip indicated it belonged to another girl." He turned to Judge Dodd. "I think Jordan can get off if he agrees to testify against Celine. And with the evidence stacked against her, including this new bank fraud charge, I think Celine will cooperate with the police rather than face those pushers. Especially if we can make a deal to reduce her sentence in exchange for her leading us to them."

Judge Dodd nodded. "I think that can be arranged. As much as I hate drug dealing of any kind, if we can prosecute the kingpins, we'll do a lot toward stamping out drugs in Sweet Valley."

Nick rose to his feet. "And this clears Jessica Wakefield?"

The judge also stood. "Yes, it does. Based on the evidence you've presented, it's obvious Jessica Wakefield was an innocent victim." The judge shook Nick's hand. "Congratulations on a job well done, Detective Fox. I'm going to recommend that you get a citation for your excellent work on this case."

Nick shrugged. "Thank you, Your Honor, but I was suspended yesterday for refusing to testify against Jessica while I searched for the real drug dealers."

Judge Dodd raised an eyebrow. "Is that so?

Well, I'll have to give the mayor a call and get that cleared up this afternoon, won't I?"

Nick grinned. "Thanks, Your Honor. I appreciate that." Nick couldn't wait to see the look on Police Chief Wallace's face when he came strolling into his office holding a big, fat cigar! *But that will come later,* he thought. *Right now it's Jessica's face I want to see, and Jessica I want to hold.*

"OK, Jessica," Mr. Mills whispered to her as the judge entered the courtroom and walked toward his bench. "We'll hope for the best, but be prepared for anything." He helped Jessica to her feet as the excited chattering in the courtroom reached a fevered pitch. Everyone was talking about Nick's surprise appearance.

Jessica took a deep breath and held it tight. Everything was happening so fast. *Has the judge accepted Nick's evidence?* she wondered, her mind racing. Was she finally going to be freed? *Or am I going back to jail?* Either way, Nick had come through for her. But was it for her or simply his duty? She felt her whole body tremble and reached out to steady herself on Mr. Mills's arm. His calming presence was the only thing keeping her from bursting.

Judge Dodd took his seat and turned, looking directly at Jessica. She felt her eyes widen and her heart begin to pound in her chest. *This is it*, she thought. *If he didn't believe Nick, then I'm finished*.

The judge rapped his gavel on the bench and the room became instantly silent. "Ladies and gentlemen of the jury," he began. "I have just received vital information regarding this case. I rule that there is not enough evidence to indict Jessica Wakefield on the charge of cocaine possession with the intent to sell."

A loud rumbling rose from the courtroom. Everyone seemed to be talking at once. Jessica's heart leaped.

The judge banged his gavel again. "Order in the court!" he demanded. "I'm not finished yet."

"Oh no," Jessica gasped, turning to Mr. Mills. "Could he be bringing me up on other charges?" Maybe it wasn't over yet.

Mr. Mills shook his head, smiling. "Let him finish."

Jessica turned back to the judge as he resumed his speech. "*The State of California versus Jessica Wakefield* is now hereby dismissed." He smiled widely. "Miss Wakefield," he said softly, "you are free to go with this court's most sincere apologies."

Jessica fell back into her chair, stunned, as the courtroom broke into loud applause. Those were the words she'd been waiting to hear since this whole mess started. *I'm free!* she thought, tears coming to her eyes. *Free at last!*

"Take your hands off me," a shrill voice screamed from the other side of the room. Jessica looked over to see Lila ripping the floppy white hat from Celine's head while the bailiff led her from the courtroom. Nick was walking directly behind them. She felt her heart swell. He hadn't abandoned her. *But does he still love me?* she wondered. *After all the trouble I caused by going to that meeting in the first place?*

Jessica remained motionless as she watched Nick make his way toward her. She felt the tears that had been brimming in her aquamarine eyes begin to flow freely down her cheeks. Nick stood before her, his dark green eyes tender and his face full of longing. She stood and opened her arms as Nick scooped her off the floor in a tight hug.

She looked up at him and time seemed to stand still as they shared a heart-stopping kiss. "Thank you, Nick," she sobbed into his soft, sweet-smelling hair. "Thank you for believing me."

Elizabeth bit her lip and sank down on the courtroom bench. All around her people were laughing, hugging Jessica, and clapping Nick on the back. But despite her joyful relief at Jessica's acquittal, she felt terrible. She had a throbbing hangover, and without the worry of Jessica's hearing, her mind was flooded with painful thoughts of Tom. She turned her face from the crowd. With all the happiness around her, she didn't want anyone to see her crying.

Elizabeth reached into the pocket of her jean jacket, looking for a tissue. Todd's lucky sweatband fell into her lap instead. She squeezed the soft, thick cotton between her slender fingers. *It worked,* she thought, smiling through her tears. *I should return it to Todd before he misses it.* She dabbed at her eyes before anyone noticed her sadness. She needed to be alone, sort out her feelings, and sleep off her hangover.

Elizabeth walked over to where Jessica was collapsed on the defendant's bench and wrapped her arms around her sister. "I'm glad everything worked out," she whispered, giving her a kiss on the cheek. "Thank Nick for me again."

"Are you leaving?" Jessica asked.

Elizabeth wrinkled her nose. "I've got to get out of these clothes. I'll see you back at our room."

Jessica smiled up at her. "Then you'll tell me all about last night, I hope. . . ." She winked. "No, you'd better save it for tomorrow. I'm planning my own late night."

Elizabeth laughed and then turned to kiss her brother and Billie good-bye.

"Liz," Alex murmured close to her. "Tom's here."

"Where?" Elizabeth asked, whipping her head around to catch a glimpse of his receding back.

Elizabeth pushed her way past Jessica's well-wishers and ran outside the courtroom.

Tom was bounding down the stairs.

Elizabeth's heart swelled. *He does care about me,* she thought. *He was at Jessica's trial to support me.*

"Tom," she cried. "Wait!" But he didn't turn. Instead he hurried down the path away from the courtroom.

"He didn't wait for me," Elizabeth whispered, swallowing her disappointment. "But he was here for me and that's what matters." Her step was lighter as she started back toward campus. Even her hangover seemed to lessen. She would call Tom as soon as she got to her room. But before she forgot, she had to return Todd's lucky sweatband.

As she walked across campus toward Todd's dorm she couldn't help wishing Tom had been at her side from the beginning. She'd missed the strong, supportive Tom she'd always counted on.

"But he *was* at the trial, Liz," she reminded herself. "In the end he did show up. I'm sure we'll be able to make up now."

230

She pushed through the doors of Todd's dorm building and headed up the stairs. Images of Tom filled her thoughts, each one more poignant than the last. Tom's dark brown eyes gazing at her tenderly, his strong arms hugging her close to him. His soft lips whispering words of love between gentle kisses.

Elizabeth smiled to herself. "When we make up, I'll have an even sweeter memory." She stepped into Todd's hall and walked toward his door. *What about Todd?* a little voice inside her teased.

"What about him?" Elizabeth muttered, blushing slightly. That had been a momentary aberration. Now that she and Tom had a chance to get back together, her feelings were back where they belonged. Tom was the keeper of her heart. Tom was who she needed to worry about.

Elizabeth reached Todd's door and knocked lightly. She tucked a strand of her blond hair behind her ear as soft footsteps approached from within. She pulled the sweatband from her pocket as Todd's door began to open. She wouldn't stay for more than a minute.

But when Todd appeared in the doorway, all thoughts of Tom flew from Elizabeth's mind. Todd stood there wearing nothing but a pair of green silk boxer shorts, his strong chest rippling with muscles. His tousled hair had fallen slightly across his forehead and his bright brown eyes were dancing. Elizabeth felt her mouth drop open as she stared at him, her heart racing. *Todd isn't only sweet, supportive, and understanding,* she thought. *He's gorgeous!*

She stepped forward and fell into his arms, the lucky sweatband slipping to the floor as her hands explored the silky, smooth skin of his powerful back. She looked up into Todd's surprised face. But before he could utter a word, she parted her lips and pulled him close, kissing him with all the sizzling passion in her soul. Her right foot found the hard edge of Todd's door and with a quick push of her foot, she closed the rest of the world off behind them.

We hope you enjoyed reading this book. If you would like to receive further information about available titles in the Bantam series, just write to the address below, with your name and address:

KIM PRIOR
Bantam Books
61–63 Uxbridge Road
London W5 5SA

If you live in Australia or New Zealand and would like more information about the series, please write to:

SALLY PORTER
Transworld Publishers (Australia) Pty Ltd
15–25 Helles Avenue
Moorebank
NSW 2170
AUSTRALIA

KIRI MARTIN
Transworld Publishers (NZ) Ltd
3 William Pickering Drive
Albany
Auckland
NEW ZEALAND

All Transworld titles are available by post from:
Bookservice by Post, PO Box 29,
Douglas, Isle of Man IM99 1BQ

Credit Cards accepted.
Please telephone 01624 675137 or fax 01624 670923
or Internet http://www.bookpost.co.uk
or e-mail: bookshop@enterprise.net for details.

Free postage and packing in the UK.
Overseas customers allow £1 per book (paperbacks)
and £3 per book (hardbacks)